S0-AQC-882

"Why don't you have a husband?" little Jenny asked,

looking up at Casey with wide, innocent eyes.

The hammer slipped from Casey's hand and hit the toe of her work boot. She swallowed—hard—marveling at the way children had of getting right to the heart of things.

"Did he go to heaven like my mommy did?"

Casey shook her head, dismissing the throbbing inside her shoe. "No. He lives in Lake Tahoe with his new wife and new baby."

The five-year-old digested this for a moment. "Daddy doesn't have a wife."

"Oh?" Casey murmured absently, rearranging her tool belt.

"I think he should marry you."

Casey stopped dead and stared at Jenny. "Whoa! What?"

"I think," Jenny repeated patiently, "that Daddy should marry *you*."

Dear Reader,

This month Silhouette Romance has six irresistible novels for you, starting with our FABULOUS FATHERS selection, *Mad for the Dad* by Terry Essig. When a sexy single man becomes an instant dad to a toddler, the independent divorcée next door offers parenthood lessons—only to dream of marriage and motherhood all over again!

In *Having Gabriel's Baby* by Kristin Morgan, our BUNDLES OF JOY book, a fleeting night of passion with a handsome, brooding rancher leaves Joelle in the family way—and the dad-to-be insisting on a marriage of convenience for the sake of the baby....

Years ago Julie had been too young for the dashing man of her dreams. Now he's back in town, and Julie's still hoping he'll make her his bride in *New Year's Wife* by Linda Varner, part of her miniseries HOME FOR THE HOLIDAYS.

What's a man to do when he has no interest in marriage but is having trouble resisting the lovely, warm and wonderful woman in his life? Get those cold feet to the nearest wedding chapel in *Family Addition* by Rebecca Daniels.

In *About That Kiss* by Jayne Addison, Joy Mackey, sister of the bride, is sure her sis's ex-fiancé has returned to sabotage the wedding. But his intention is to walk down the aisle with Joy!

And finally, when a woman shows up on a bachelor doctor's doorstep with a baby that looks just like him, everyone in town mistakenly thinks the tiny tot is his in Christine Scott's *Groom on the Loose*.

Enjoy!

Melissa Senate, Senior Editor

Please address questions and book requests to:
Silhouette Reader Service
U.S.: 3010 Walden Ave., P.O. Box 1325, Buffalo, NY 14269
Canadian: P.O. Box 609, Fort Erie, Ont. L2A 5X3

FAMILY ADDITION

Rebecca Daniels

Silhouette®
ROMANCE™
Published by Silhouette Books
America's Publisher of Contemporary Romance

If you purchased this book without a cover you should be aware that this book is stolen property. It was reported as "unsold and destroyed" to the publisher, and neither the author nor the publisher has received any payment for this "stripped book."

TYVMFE!
For Georgia Bockoven
and Sharon Brevik.
Thanks for all the love and support,
and for having broad shoulders
even without shoulder pads!

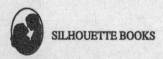 SILHOUETTE BOOKS

ISBN 0-373-19201-0

FAMILY ADDITION

Copyright © 1997 by Ann Marie Fattarsi

All rights reserved. Except for use in any review, the reproduction or utilization of this work in whole or in part in any form by any electronic, mechanical or other means, now known or hereafter invented, including xerography, photocopying and recording, or in any information storage or retrieval system, is forbidden without the written permission of the editorial office, Silhouette Books, 300 East 42nd Street, New York, NY 10017 U.S.A.

All characters in this book have no existence outside the imagination of the author and have no relation whatsoever to anyone bearing the same name or names. They are not even distantly inspired by any individual known or unknown to the author, and all incidents are pure invention.

This edition published by arrangement with Harlequin Books S.A.

® and TM are trademarks of Harlequin Books S.A., used under license. Trademarks indicated with ® are registered in the United States Patent and Trademark Office, the Canadian Trade Marks Office and in other countries.

Printed in U.S.A.

REBECCA DANIELS

will never forget the first time she read a Silhouette novel. "I was at my sister's house, sitting by the pool and trying without much success to get interested in the book I'd brought from home. Everything seemed to distract me—the dog, the kids, the sea gulls. Finally, my sister plucked the book from my hands, told me she was going to give me something I wouldn't be able to put down and handed me my first Silhouette novel. Guess what? She was right! For that lazy afternoon by her pool, I will forever be grateful." From that day on, Rebecca has been writing romance novels and loving every minute of it.

Born in the Midwest but raised in Southern California, she now resides in the scenic coastal community of Santa Barbara with her two sons. She loves early-morning walks along the beach, an occasional round of golf, and hearing from her fans. You can write Rebecca in care of Silhouette Books, 300 East 42nd St., New York, NY 10017.

Chapter One

"Casey, huh?" Colt muttered. He massaged his forehead, feeling the tension build between his eyes.

"Yeah, Casey," Jenny said, her excited breath blowing heavily into the phone. "And Casey says the window seat will have room enough for all my stuffed animals—even all the unicorns."

"Is that right, all of them, huh?" Colt mumbled, leaning back against the headboard of the bed, which actually wasn't a headboard at all but rather a piece of carved, molded wood mounted to the wall of his generic-looking motel room. He closed his eyes and rubbed at the lids, picturing his five-year-old daughter in his mind with her big blue eyes and fine, silky blond hair. He could just imagine her at home, sitting in his easy chair and holding the telephone to her ear with both hands. "This Casey seems to know a lot."

"Oh, yeah." Jenny giggled, excited. "Casey's real smart. And Casey says the shelves will be big enough for all my books, too. Casey says it'll make a great place for storytime—my own private place." Jenny stopped just long enough for another little giggle and to catch a quick breath. "When my room's finished, can we start reading my bedtime story there, Daddy? Can we, please? Casey says it would be a perfect place for a bedtime story. Can we read it there? Can we, Daddy? Please?"

Colt scowled. Casey, Casey, Casey. After five days, he'd heard all he wanted about this character Casey. Just who was this guy, anyway? It wasn't like it was *Casey's* idea to put a bay window with a window seat in Jenny's new room. He'd come up with that idea on his own—only now, it was Casey taking the credit.

Sullivan Construction had come highly recommended, which is why he'd hired them to build the addition on to his ranch house in the first place. Bob Sullivan had assured him they employed the best workers in the industry. Colt would have liked to stick around home to find out, but construction on the house had begun the day he'd left San Andreas to attend the California Horseman's Convention at the Earl Warren Show Grounds in Santa Barbara.

But it wasn't exactly the quality of the work that he was concerned with right now. It was the workers themselves—or rather, one worker in particular. Casey. The guy had made one hell of an impression on Jenny.

"We'll have plenty of time to decide all that later," he said, putting her off. "Is Emma close by?"

"Yeah, she's right here," Jenny said, glancing up at the housekeeper sitting on the arm of the chair beside her. Only she wasn't ready to relinquish the telephone just yet. There were so many more things she wanted to talk about—so many more things about Casey. "But I forgot to tell you about the big truck that was here today and the ride Casey gave me in the wheelbarrow."

"You can tell me about that tomorrow," he assured her. "Let me talk to Emma now."

"But, Daddy, don't you want to hear about the lumber?" Jenny persisted. "And the cement mixer?"

"Of course I do, honey, but it's already past your bedtime. When I call tomorrow, I want you to tell me all about them then, okay?"

"But Casey says it's okay to stay up late during the summer," Jenny complained. "Casey says that's what kids are suppose to do."

Colt's frown deepened, and he felt his blood pressure edge up a degree. Casey says, Casey says. He was getting a little tired of hearing about what Casey said. Only he didn't want to do anything that would upset Jenny, or hurt her feelings. There would be time when he got home to deal with this Casey character, so he did what he could to keep the annoyance out of his voice.

"Well," he said, pushing aside his displeasure. "Why don't we let Casey stick to construction and let me decide what's best for you, okay?"

"Okay, Daddy," Jenny agreed, standing up and balancing herself carefully on the cushion of the chair.

"But I want you to come home. I don't like it when you're away."

"I don't like it much, either. But it's just for a few more days."

"I miss you."

"I miss you, too, baby."

"Tell me how many more."

"Okay, fingers ready?" he asked, going through what had become a nightly ritual for them.

"Ready."

"Hold up two."

"Two," she mumbled into the receiver.

"Got them?" he asked, imagining her delicate little hands and feeling the emotion rise up in his chest. "Two fingers?"

"Uh-huh," she said. "Two fingers."

"Okay, now that's how many nights. Two."

Jenny studied her two fingers, making a little waving motion with them. "Two fingers."

"Two nights," Colt repeated. "And then I won't have to be gone anywhere for a long time."

Jenny dropped one finger and then the other. "Two more. Promise?"

"I promise."

"Yea!" Jenny cheered with a giggle, satisfied. "Oh! And, Daddy, did I tell you about—"

"Jen," Colt said sternly, interrupting her. "I know what you're doing, and it's not going to work. Enough stalling. Give the phone to Emma and get to bed."

"All right," she groused glumly. "'Night, Daddy."

"Good night, sweetheart," Colt said, smiling. He sat up, listening as Jenny handed the telephone to their housekeeper and laughing at the exchange that followed.

"That's enough of that, young lady." He heard Emma's voice in the background. "You'll not be using that chair as a trampoline."

Colt's smile grew wider, hearing Jenny's impish giggle and Emma Parker's exasperated sigh. It didn't seem to matter how reproving Emma tried to sound, or how many threats she made, Jenny knew she had the stout housekeeper wrapped around her little finger—and most of the time took full advantage.

"Hello there, C.W.," Emma said to him over the line. "Did you hear the way that child of yours talks to me?"

"I heard, I heard." Colt laughed, also hearing the affection in Emma's voice. "Everything going all right?"

"Of course," Emma sighed, assuring him. "What about you? I hope you're taking some time to enjoy yourself a little, getting out and meeting...folks. Not just work, work, work."

Folks. Colt's smile widened. That was Emma's not-so-subtle way of asking about women. What she really wanted to know was if he'd met any interesting *women* yet? Emma had decided it was time for him to marry again. As far as she was concerned, he'd lived alone long enough, and Jenny needed a new mother. He, on the other hand, happened to disagree. He and Jenny were just fine, and as far as he was concerned, a woman was the last thing they needed in their lives.

"Oh," he said, being purposely evasive. "I take a break from time to time."

"Good," Emma said, knowing him well enough to know that was as much as she was going to get from him.

"Emma," Colt said, the smile slowly fading from his lips. "What's up with the construction? How's it looking to you?"

"Oh, I think you'll be pleased," Emma said excitedly. "Of course, everything's a mess around here, but they really seem to be moving things along. It's only been a couple of days, but you should see the difference."

"Jenny keeps mentioning this...this Casey," Colt said approaching the subject carefully. "As a matter of fact, that's all she talks about. She's really taken with this character. Is this something I should be worried about? I don't like her getting too friendly with strangers."

Emma laughed. "Believe me when I tell you, C.W., I don't think you've got anything to worry about from Casey."

Colt considered this, feeling a tight band of tension around his head. If there was one thing he knew he could depend on, it was Emma. She loved Jenny nearly as much as he did, and normally he would trust her judgment completely. But Emma wasn't immune to a little sweet talk herself—and this Casey definitely sounded like he could sweet talk the ladies.

"Well," he murmured, rubbing at a sensitive spot in the middle of his forehead. "Do me a favor and keep your eyes open, okay?"

"I always do," Emma assured him patiently. "You know I'm not going to let anyone near that precious little bundle who isn't okay. Relax, and quit worrying will you?''

"Quit worrying," Colt mumbled dryly, taking what comfort he could from Emma's reassuring words. "As if that was possible."

"No, I suppose it isn't," Emma said with a sigh. "But that's just part of being a daddy now, isn't it?" She chuckled. "Get some rest, C.W. Your little girl is fine, and you're sounding kind of punchy."

Punchy. Colt had to smile. Maybe he was punchy, maybe that's what had him feeling vulnerable about the four hundred miles that separated him from his home and his daughter.

After a mumbled good-night to Emma, he hung up the phone, feeling another swell of emotion rise in his chest. Colton Wyatt didn't like being away—from Jenny, or from the Cache Creek Ranch. But attending the convention was mandatory for the president of the Mother Lode Horsemen's Association. As longtime president of the MLHA, Colt had big plans for their local association, and the contacts he made each year at the annual conference had gone a long way in helping him make those plans a reality.

The MLHA hosted an annual horse show competition each year and Colt hoped to take it out of the amateur circuit and turn it into a first-rate, statewide event. It was an ambitious project, one that both he and the other MLHA board members had worked on long and hard—meeting state and local ordinances, making contact with the appropriate breeding and show associations and seeking the funding they needed to expand and update their facilities. Such an event would be a boon to area stables and breeders, not only allowing them a premier showcase for their stock, but expanding their impact and influence in the industry.

Just thinking of the work that still needed to be done caused the tension between Colt's eyes to grow worse. He rubbed a tired hand over his eyes, drawing in a deep breath and stretching his aching muscles. He felt stiff and sore—more like he'd spent a day in the saddle instead of talking business and networking with other breeders and ranchers.

And frankly, he'd talked enough business for one day. He'd had his fill of discussing the pros and cons of the latest computerized stud registry or debating the new county restrictions on show ground permits and trying to get a handle on the controversy surrounding state licensing fees. He just wanted to clear his mind of all those troubling things and take a hot shower, wanted to clean his tired body and crawl into bed and try to get the picture of a seedy construction worker hanging around his little girl out of his mind.

Colt thought of Emma and how she'd advised him not to worry, but that was asking the impossible. Worrying about Jenny was simply something he did—like breathing or eating. It just came naturally—something he couldn't control.

He reached for the small bottle of over-the-counter pain relievers on the nightstand beside him. Business, on the other hand, was something he could control, something he could push to the back of his brain and deal with when he wanted. Maybe that was why he'd become so good at it, why he'd succeeded where so many others had failed.

Colt hadn't gotten interested in ranching, hadn't become involved in breeding horses and show competitions because of his interest in business. He'd just been a kid who loved to ride horses.

He'd only been seven when his parents were killed and he'd gone to live with his Uncle Sid and Aunt Mary on their small ranch in Calavaras County. But he had been old enough to know what he liked, and he'd liked horses. He'd liked riding them, grooming them and learning all about them. It hadn't taken him long to realize that modern ranching and the world of horseflesh and breeding was a business—a tough, demanding business that tended to chew ranchers up and spit them out. Still, he'd managed to survive by being prepared and by learning everything about the business—inside and out.

Today Cache Creek Ranch was a success by any standards, providing him with a comfortable living and known for its fine breed of Appaloosa. And just because he went to work every day wearing cowboy boots and jeans instead of Italian-made loafers and a three-piece suit, Colt had never lost sight of the fact that he didn't just run a ranch, he ran a business.

Somehow, for a kid who'd started out just loving horses, he'd turned out to be a pretty good businessman.

Colt swallowed two tablets, washing down their powdery bitterness with a swig of the lukewarm water left in a glass earlier in the day. Leaning forward, he pulled off his boots, catching a glimpse of himself in the mirror on the wall. He didn't look much like a prosperous businessman. Tonight he just looked like one tired cowpoke—and that was exactly how he felt.

Rising slowly to his feet, Colt peeled off his shirt and socks and tossed them carelessly to the floor. He waited until the steam from the shower stall was billowing out of the bathroom in huge, wet clouds before he dropped his jeans to the floor and stepped beneath the hot stream.

Closing his eyes, he let the scalding water flow over him, feeling his stiff, aching muscles begin to loosen and relax. This was what he needed—this, and a good night's sleep. It wasn't that he minded attending the conference every year. Actually, he'd come to look forward to it. Santa Barbara was a beautiful city, and the Earl Warren Show Grounds was a first rate facility. It was his one opportunity during the year to get out and socialize, to break from his normal routine and mingle just a little. Ever since Karen's death, a social life was something he hadn't thought much about.

Colt opened his eyes, reaching for the bar of soap in the dish and rubbing it briskly between the palms of his hands. He didn't like thinking about his wife, or about the way his life had been when she'd been alive. Of course, if he hadn't met Karen, there would be no Jenny, and for that reason alone he could never say he had regrets. But the rest of it...

The rest of it he would just as soon forget. He'd known when he'd met Karen that she had some serious problems. Her childhood had been difficult, and she'd grown up feeling unloved and unwanted. But her instability and insecurities went far deeper than he'd ever suspected. He probably should have seen the signs—probably should have been able to predict her problems with alcohol and her brush with prescription drugs, but he hadn't. And by the time he had realized just how troubled Karen was, just how deep her problems went, it had been too late. Their hasty marriage hadn't allowed time for second thoughts or introspection.

Of course now, looking back, it all seemed so clear to him. Karen had manipulated him from the beginning, just like she'd manipulated everything in her life. She had plotted how she would get him to marry her like a writer plotting a book—only this story hadn't ended very well.

Colt let the water cascade over him, sending a million tiny rivulets cutting pathways through the lather of suds that covered his chest. He thought of Jenny and how happy he'd been on the day she was born. When he'd looked at his little daughter, when he'd held her in his arms, it hadn't mattered that Karen had tricked him into marrying her. At that moment, just having Jenny was enough. He'd been too happy, too caught up in the moment to consider what kind of impact Karen's manipulative nature might have on their child. He'd wanted to think everything would be different, wanted to believe motherhood would change her, would make her whole, but he'd been a fool.

The hot water had turned tepid, and Colt reached for the faucet and turned it off. He stepped out of the shower, patting himself dry and wrapping the damp towel around his waist. He walked back to the bed, turning off lights as he went, and fell back on the mattress. He felt exhausted and drained. Only this time the fatigue had a lot less to do with the long day he had, and more to do with the miserable memories of his marriage.

Colt looked forward to the time he could think about Karen and not feel drained and frustrated, but it hadn't happened yet. Maybe in time it would, maybe in time he would be able to put all the pain behind him, all the bad feelings aside. But two years had passed since she'd driven her car off a bridge and into the swollen Mokulumme River, and it hadn't happened yet.

Colt closed his eyes, trying to picture Karen in his head, but her image was fuzzy. He fumbled with the towel, pulling it free and tossing it to the floor. He reached for the sheet, pulling it up over his naked body.

He and Jenny had moved on with their lives. Jenny didn't even ask him about Karen anymore. Hopefully she'd forgotten all those awful episodes with her mother—the yelling and the screaming, the desperate threats. Jenny seemed content to know that Mommy now lived with the angels, and hopefully she would never have to know the truth, never have to know how her mother had used her to get what she'd wanted.

Colt's mind shifted to the construction worker again, and suddenly he felt wide awake. He'd always made an effort to see that Jenny had plenty of people in her life—friends, family, playmates. It wasn't like Jenny to just latch on to someone, a stranger, and he couldn't help but be concerned. He was determined no one was ever going to use his daughter again.

* * *

"Casey! Hey, Casey!"

Catching a glimpse of Jenny standing in the yard below, Casey stepped back, carefully moving around Ronnie as he tore through what was left of the upstairs bedroom wall with a powerful circular saw. Motioning for Jenny to stay where she was, Casey climbed down the makeshift scaffolding, taking the last three feet in one jump.

"I thought you promised you wouldn't come this close unless you had my permission."

Jenny looked sheepish, twisting a small satin ribbon in her hand. "But I thought this was the safety zone."

Casey reached up and pulled off the bright yellow hard hat, allowing a mass of long, brown hair to tumble out. "Give me your hand, and I'll show you one more time where the safety zone stops. But you have to remember this time, okay? Promise?"

"I promise," Jenny said with a nod, slipping her small hand into Casey's bigger gloved one.

Cassandra Sullivan, or "Casey" as she was known to just about everyone who knew her, had been around construction sites her whole life. But she could still remember the times her father had taken her by the hand and they had paced off the "safety zone" together. It had been Buck Sullivan's only way of keeping her out of the way and out of danger, when he wasn't there to do that himself. Of course, on those rare times when she had forgotten, when she'd gotten too close, Buck hadn't hesitated to give her a good talking to—which usually included being left at home

and banished from going to work with him for at least
a week. Casey had been willing to do just about anything to avoid being left behind, even if that meant
staying in the "zone."

Unfortunately that wasn't an option she had with
little Jenny Wyatt. She couldn't exactly banish the little girl from her own house. Jenny's father had hired
them to put an addition onto his house, not discipline
his daughter. Still, she had a responsibility. Even
though she'd never actually met Colton Wyatt, Casey
suspected he wouldn't appreciate it if his daughter ac-
cidentally got hurt.

"It's very important," Casey said, as she and Jenny
walked hand in hand across the lawn. "*Very important* to remember that a construction site is not a place
to play." They paced off a wide rectangle around the
house, setting the boundaries and drawing imaginary
lines. "I know there are all kinds of things lying
around that look interesting—tools, equipment, supplies. Things that look like they might be fun to play
with," she said, giving Jenny the same speech her father had given to her on more than one occasion. They
reached the paved drive that led around the ranch
house to where her pickup truck was parked. "But
they're not toys, and they could be very dangerous to
someone who doesn't know how to use them. There
are sharp edges on some of them, or they're heavy and
could fall and smash a toe." Casey stopped and knelt
down, taking both of Jenny's hands in hers. "And you
know, I'd feel really bad if you got hurt on my construction site. Please try to remember the safety zone
and not come too close. Okay?"

"Okay," Jenny said in a quiet voice.

Casey looked into Jenny's large, sad eyes and felt a pang of guilt. She didn't exactly like being the heavy any more than she liked risking an accident.

Just then an idea popped into her head. Rising quickly to her feet, she headed for her truck, pulling off her gloves and tucking them into the rear pocket of her jeans. "You know what? I just thought of something."

"What?" Jenny asked, watching her with wide eyes.

"I've got this job I need to do, but I need some help. Would you be interested?"

"A job?" Jenny's eyes grew wide with excitement. "Sure."

Casey searched through the large toolboxes in the bed of her truck. After a few minutes, she pulled out a big spool of yellow tape. Printed over and over along the length of the tape in bold black letters were the words: Construction Area, Do Not Enter.

"Here, you carry this," she said, handing Jenny the spool. "We need to make this safety zone official."

They walked to the large scrub oak at the end of the drive. Jenny took one end of the tape and circled the massive tree trunk. She handed the end back to Casey, who tied the tape into a knot. Then, holding the spool between them, they stretched a line of bright yellow tape along the imaginary line they had just paced off. They retraced their steps, stringing the tape in their wake and cordoning off the construction site, separating it from the rest of the yard.

"There," Casey said after they'd roped off an area that wouldn't put Jenny any closer than fifteen feet of any activity. "What do you think?"

"Wow," Jenny said, looking out across the yard. "It looks pretty."

Casey laughed, kneeling down and resting her hands lightly on Jenny's slender shoulders. "Well, I don't know about pretty, but at least we won't forget where the safety zone starts and stops." She plunked a finger on Jenny's nose and stood up. "Thanks for the help."

"Sure, I liked it," Jenny said, smiling. She held up the spool of tape, which was considerably smaller now.

Casey shook her head. "No, you keep it. Maybe you can think of a few more places that might need roping off."

"Okay," Jenny said excitedly. She turned and stared back at her house. "Maybe I should put some on the back porch. You know, cause Emma might forget and try and come out. Or the back walk, so Molly won't get hurt when she comes over to play."

"Sounds great." Casey smiled, imagining the yellow caution tape would probably start showing up in all kinds of places. She took a deep breath, gazing back up at the house as she pulled the gloves from her rear pocket and slipped them on. Ronnie had just finished cutting through the last section of wall, exposing the upstairs hall to the outside sun. She reached for her yellow hard hat, twining her long hair into a ponytail and stashing it up inside. "Well, back to work," she said, glancing down at Jenny. "Tell you what. You be good and stay in the safety zone, and I'll take you up to the second floor and let you look through a peephole I found that looks right into the kitchen before I go home tonight. Is that a deal?''

Jenny's mouth twisted into a frown. "But Daddy says I shouldn't spy on people 'cause it's not polite.''

"Well,'' Casey said, considering this. "He's right. But we'll tell Emma first. That way, if she's in the kitchen she'll know we'll be looking. I don't think it's spying when the person you're looking at knows you're looking. Deal?''

"Deal,'' Jenny said, her face breaking into a grin. "Thanks, Casey.'' She looked down at the spool of yellow tape in her hands. "Boy, wait till I tell Daddy.''

Casey laughed as she watched Jenny run up the gentle slope toward the drive and disappear around the corner of the house. She didn't know who this Colton Wyatt was, but he had one terrific little girl.

"A spool of what?''

Jenny took a deep breath, too impatient to try to explain. "Long yellow stuff, and I put it across the driveway and along the sidewalk and also by the basement door. It's to keep us safe. Oh, and, Daddy, Casey took me upstairs and I looked through a peephole in the floor, and guess what? I could see Emma in the kitchen.''

Colt felt the tension building across his eyes, and he clenched his jaw down tight. First a spool of long yellow stuff, and now a spy hole. Just what the hell kind of construction was this guy doing to his house, anyway?

"A peephole?" he muttered darkly. "You know what I've said about spying on people."

"I know, I know. It's not polite. But we didn't spy, honest. We told Emma we were watching, and it's not spying when the person you're watching knows you're watching them. Casey just let me poke my finger into it."

"Oh, fine," Colt grumbled again, shaking his head. "Just poked fingers." He sat for another fifteen minutes while Jenny rattled on, not having the heart to tell her he'd heard all he wanted about Casey. He would be going home tomorrow, and he'd put a stop to all of this soon enough. He'd take care of this Casey character once and for all.

Chapter Two

"There's Casey," Jenny squealed, jumping up and down on the porch and waving frantically.

Colt peered over the top of his newspaper, watching as the mud-spattered pickup pulled off the highway and rumbled up the drive. It was about time, he thought as he leisurely reached for his coffee mug from the small table beside the porch swing. He wasn't about to be hurried, wasn't about to rush down the driveway in eager anticipation no matter how anxious he was to finally meet this character face-to-face. The guy had kept him waiting long enough. The other two workers had been toiling away for well over an hour now. Apparently this Casey was able to keep banker's hours.

As the truck rolled to a stop at the end of the drive, Jenny leapt down the porch steps. Colt scowled as he watched his daughter sprinting down the walk that skirted the porch and led around the house toward the drive. Since he'd walked through the door last night, all he'd heard was Casey this, and Casey that. Jenny had actually been so excited about the idea of him finally meeting Casey, she'd had a hard time falling asleep.

Colt shook his head, swallowing the last of his coffee in one gulp. He didn't know what kind of spell this character had put on her, but he was going to put a stop to it—right now.

Crumpling the newspaper and tossing it down onto the swing beside him, he stood up. He could see Casey sitting behind the wheel, wearing a yellow hard hat and smiling out at Jenny as she ran down the walk toward the truck. The guy was either unbelievably brazen, or very sure of himself. Did he think because he had Jenny and Emma wrapped around his little finger he could do whatever the hell he wanted, he could show up for work over an hour late and no one would notice?

Colt stepped down from the porch, carrying the empty coffee mug with him. If the guy thought he could pull the same kind of nonsense with him, he had another think coming.

As he made his way down the walk, Colt saw Casey open the door and step out of the truck. He was surprised to see how small the guy was—and how skinny, too. In his mind he'd pictured Casey as big and burly—like the co-workers who had shown up earlier. But Casey wasn't anything like that. He was thin and lean—built almost like a wom—

Colt stopped dead in his tracks, the coffee mug slipping soundlessly from his hand, landing in the grass with a soft thud. Casey had just reached up and pulled the yellow hard hat off, sending long, brown tresses spilling down her back.

A woman?

There had to be some kind of mistake. How could she...how could this woman be Casey?

"Mr. Wyatt, hello," Casey said, extending her hand to the sandy-haired man standing on the walk staring at her like she'd just dropped out of the sky. "I'm Cassandra Sullivan. It's nice to finally meet you."

"Come on, Daddy," Jenny urged, grabbing her father's hand and pulling him the rest of the way down the walk. "This is Casey. *Casey.*"

"Casey," Colt mumbled, as Jenny tugged at his arm. The woman was about as far from the burly construction worker he'd expected as she could get, and his mind was having trouble computing.

"She's right," Casey laughed, conceding the point with a shrug. "Everyone calls me Casey. It's a...a nickname."

Colt took Casey's outstretched hand, but heard little of what she said. The ringing in his ears was too loud, too distracting.

"Casey," he murmured again, feeling her warm, soft hand in his and trying to think if he'd ever seen eyes as clear or as dark as hers. "You're...you're Casey."

Casey looked up into Colt's deep blue eyes and felt gooseflesh rise along her arms. For days she'd listened while Jenny had talked on and on about her daddy—what he liked and the things he did. Jenny had painted him out to be such a wonderful father, Casey had just started picturing him as her own father had been—comfortable looking with a paunchy middle and balding head.

Colton Wyatt looked nothing like that.

"Jenny's told me so much about you I feel as though we've already met," Casey said quickly, pulling her hand free of his. "She's a wonderful little girl. You should be very proud."

"Yes...yes, she's something all right," Colt sighed, glancing down into his daughter's upturned face. What could Jenny have possibly said that had him thinking her friend, Casey, was a man?

"I believe you met my brother when he came to do the estimate," Casey continued. "Bobby. He runs our front office."

"Bobby," Colt repeated, giving his head a little shake. "Bob Sullivan?"

"Yes, Bob," Casey said, regarding him carefully. The way he was looking at her made her uneasy, and she took an unsteady step backward. Clearing her throat, she turned and gestured toward the construction. "So, what do you think?"

What did he think? What did he *think?* He thought he had to be some kind of idiot. He'd been ready to charge down the driveway and start issuing orders and discharging ultimatums, and she'd stepped out of that truck wearing a yellow hard hat and tight-fitting jeans and completely taken the wind from his sails.

He turned and stared up at the exposed beams along the back of his house, trying to picture her wielding a hammer or working a saw.

"I think it looks like there's a lot of work to do," he said after a moment.

"You're right about that," Casey said, taking a deep breath. She pointed to the stack of lumber and the huge sheets of drywall and siding piled along the side of the garage. "But we can be grateful we've managed to get the bulk of our supplies delivered on time. That's always a good sign. Nothing's worse than sitting around with a crew and not having any materials for them to work with." She gave Ronnie a wave when he looked up from his hammer gun. "We'll finish up the framework for the foundation today. I've got Valley Concrete coming Friday to pour the foundation. That will give us the whole weekend to let it set up. On Monday we can start framing the walls and not really have any down time. You'll start to see it take shape after that."

Colt listened as she explained about plumbing routes and electrical switches, noticing how slender and delicate her hands were as she pointed and gestured. They weren't callused and hard as he'd expected, but rather soft and very feminine.

"Bob assured me everything would be finished and completed in eight to ten weeks—time for us to get Jenny settled into her room before kindergarten starts in the fall," he said, almost thinking he could smell the soft fragrance of her hair. "I hope that's still what we're looking at."

Casey cringed inwardly and banked down a sudden wave of anxiety. Bobby had gotten them into trouble before, making promises that were impossible to keep, and they'd nearly lost everything because of it. It had taken her years of careful planning and painstaking work to put all that behind them. She didn't even want to think what it might mean if he were to start all that again.

"We're sure going to try, Mr. Wyatt," she said as diplomatically as she could. "Of course, keep in mind there are always things that can come up unexpectedly to slow you down—supply shortages, shipping delays, bad weather. But don't worry, I'm going to do everything I can to get you settled before September." She hesitated a moment, then gave her hands a clap. "Well, I guess that's about it. Oh, wait—" She stopped suddenly, tapping a hand against the front pocket of her shirt. Reaching inside, she pulled out a folded manila envelope. "I almost forgot. I had to swing by the county recorder's office this morning to file some amended plans on the electrical, which is why I'm so late. Anyway, I picked this up for you."

Colt took the yellow envelope from her, peering inside. "For me?"

"Yeah," she said, winding her long hair around her hand and tucking it up inside the hard hat again. "It's your copy of the building permit. Thought it would save you a trip down to pick it up."

"Oh," Colt mumbled, remembering how he'd been ready to accuse him—her—of keeping bankers' hours. "I see, thank you."

"No problem," she said, quickly looking away. She wasn't exactly sure why, but she seemed to have gotten off on the wrong foot with this man and it made her very uncomfortable. The last thing Sullivan Construction needed was a disgruntled customer, especially when the job had just begun. "Well, I'd better get to work before Jake and Ronnie start thinking I've deserted them." Turning to Jenny, she gave her a wink. "Picnic today?"

"You bet," Jenny giggled. "And Daddy's coming, too. Isn't that great?"

The smile on Casey's lips stiffened just a little. Actually it wasn't okay at all. Actually the thought of eating her lunch with Colton Wyatt looking at her like she was a bug under a microscope didn't appeal to her at all, but she forced herself to smile wider. "Great, the more the merrier. And remember what you promised."

"I remember, I remember," Jenny groused playfully, knowing the routine they went through every morning. "Stay in the zone."

Casey laughed, reaching into the back of her truck and pulling out her leather tool belt. Slipping it around her waist, she reached for the pair of leather gloves that were tucked in a rear pocket of her jeans.

"Again, Mr. Wyatt, it was nice meeting you," she said in her best public relations voice as she extended her free hand to him one more time. "I'll be around if you think of any questions, or just want to know what's going on. Please, don't hesitate to ask."

"Don't worry, I won't," Colt said abruptly, taking her hand. There was something about the way her hand felt in his that he found unsettling, that made him uneasy and had the words coming out sharper than he'd intended.

"Yes . . . well, good," Casey said, her words faltering just a little. She gave them a small wave, then turned and started away.

Colt watched as she ducked beneath the yellow caution tape and started to work. She was far from petite—her tall, lean frame had to stand five foot seven or better. But working with her two brawny crew members, she looked small and delicate.

"What's the zone?" he asked Jenny while his gaze followed Casey as she moved through the construction site.

"The *zone,*" Jenny explained impatiently, pointing to the long line of tape strung out across the yard. "The safety zone. Don't you remember? I told you on the telephone. Me and Casey made it."

Colt nodded, remembering Jenny chattering on about something to do with yellow tape. He hadn't paid much attention at the time. He'd been too preoccupied with concern over his daughter spending so much time with a strange man.

He watched as Casey bent down and picked up a huge circular saw with an ease that seemed to defy her slender arms. But there was nothing "manly" about Casey Sullivan. Despite the tools hanging from her belt, despite the boots and the jeans and the yellow hard hat, she was all woman. Any man within eyeshot could see that.

Still, she was a stranger, and she'd formed a bond with Jenny, and that was reason enough to remain leery. Jenny had been used before to get a selfish woman what she wanted, and he wasn't about to ever let that happen again.

"So where's your dad?" Casey asked, smoothing out the picnic blanket that she'd placed under a tree in Jenny's backyard. "I thought he was going to have lunch with us?"

"He got busy," Jenny said, plunking herself down across from Casey. She popped a seedless grape into her mouth. "Mountain Lady is going to have a baby, and the vet was coming today." Jenny picked another couple of grapes from the bunch and crammed them into her cheek. "Mountain Lady is Daddy's favorite horse. He worries about her a lot. Once, when it was raining and really dark outside, he got out of bed and..."

Casey leaned back against the tree trunk, taking a bite of sandwich and listening as Jenny chattered on about her father and a storm and a night he'd spent in the stables. She couldn't help feeling relieved. At least now she could relax and enjoy her lunch, wouldn't have to worry about the piercing blue gaze of Colt Wyatt watching her every move.

As Jenny talked, Casey let her mind drift, thinking back to the awkward encounter they'd had in the drive. It wasn't anger she'd seen in his eyes, nothing hostile or rancorous—not exactly, anyway. But there had been no warmth, either. Jenny was such a friendly little girl, so outgoing and open. Casey had expected her father to be the same.

Only there had been nothing friendly or welcoming in the greeting he'd given her this morning. Was he suspicious of everyone he met, or was there just something about her he didn't like? Did he have something against female construction workers, or did he just have it in for all women in general?

Casey considered this. Jenny had talked about her mother—her mother who lived in Heaven and played with the angels. Of course that would mean Colt Wyatt was a widower, and for that reason alone she should probably cut the guy some slack. After all, it seemed reasonable that a parent left to raise a child alone would be protective. But why did he want to protect his daughter from her? What threat could she possibly pose to Jenny? What threat did she pose to him?

"Casey? Do you want to?"

Casey jumped, and gave her head a shake. "I'm sorry, sweetie, what did you say?"

"Go riding," Jenny repeated, rising to her knees. "In the buggy. Daddy and me go all the time. Wanna come sometime?"

Casey made a face, thinking that idea sounded about as inviting as the three of them having lunch together had. "Oh, thanks, sweetheart, but I don't think so. I don't really know much about horses. To be honest, I've never really been on a horse—except when I was little and my dad would take me to the pony rides at the county fair."

"But it's easy," Jenny insisted, scooting across the blanket on her knees. "I can teach you. Daddy will, too."

The picture of Colt Wyatt helping her up onto the back of a horse wasn't exactly the enticement she knew Jenny had hoped it would be, but Casey didn't have the heart to turn the child down completely.

"Well, we'll see. Maybe sometime," she conceded vaguely. "But right now, I've got to get back to work." She gathered up the remains of her lunch, cramming it back into her lunch pail. Picking up the package of pink and white coconut-covered cupcakes, she offered them to Jenny. "Here, dessert's on me. And don't forget to finish your milk."

"Wow," Jenny said, her eyes widening with delight. "Thanks."

Casey smiled as she watched Jenny bite through the marshmallow frosting and into the chocolate cake. It was obvious she took delight in the unexpected treat, smacking her lips and savoring the gooey richness of the cake.

Casey couldn't help wondering, as she started back across the lawn toward the work site, what it was about growing up that made you forget the simple pleasures. Cookies and milk, walks in the park, kisses at bedtime—children understood and appreciated those treasures. They didn't take joy for granted, hadn't yet learned how to skim over or put things off. They knew what it was to enjoy life, knew how to recognize and regard what they had while they had it.

Casey hopped over the wooden framing that would soon hold the concrete foundation of the new wing. Wasn't that really what it was all about? Wasn't that the real magic of parent and child? That through your

children you remembered, through them you learned
to appreciate the simple pleasures again?

Casey felt an overwhelming sense of sadness de-
scend upon her. She glanced back at Jenny, watching
as the little girl licked her sticky fingers and reached
for her thermos of milk. Did Colt Wyatt remember
and appreciate when he looked at his little girl? Would
her own lost child have helped her to remember, too?

Casey bent down, picking up her tool belt and
strapping it around her waist. It had been years since
she'd taken that fall, since the child in her womb had
been lost. The tears had come and gone, the grief and
mourning had long since passed. And yet she still remembered, she still looked back and wondered about
what might have been.

Charlie had never forgiven her for losing the baby
they both had wanted so desperately, but she could
hardly blame him. She hadn't been able to forgive
herself, either. Charlie had worked for her father for
years, and he understood better than anyone how
quickly accidents could happen at a construction site.
And of course she should have listened.

From the day she and Charlie had walked down the
aisle, she couldn't wait to start a family. When she'd
discovered that a baby was on the way, she'd thought
all her dreams had come true. So why hadn't she
stayed away from the construction site? Why hadn't
she taken a desk job in the office as Charlie and her
father had wanted her to?

But she'd never been content to sit back and watch,
to stay on the sidelines when there was work to be

done. Stubbornly, she'd convinced herself that she could be careful, she could continue to work—for a short time anyway—and stay out of harm's way.

What a fool she had been. She should have known it was impossible to guard against everything. In the end it had been a simple misstep, a silly little slip from a scaffolding that shouldn't have meant anything at all. But to a woman in her seventh week of pregnancy, it had meant everything.

Charlie had tried, she knew that. He'd tried to get beyond it, tried to put the hurt and the anger behind him. But in the end it had proved too much. Six months after she'd lost the baby, Charlie left, slipping out of town and out of her life forever.

Casey pulled the hammer free of the loop on her belt, bending down and pounding an errant nail into place. There had been damage from the fall, and the doctors had said there might be problems with her conceiving again. Her dreams of a home and a family didn't look very good.

But she didn't like thinking about all of that, about all she'd had and all she'd lost. It had all happened such a long time ago—a lifetime really. The pain had subsided, the scars had healed, her life had moved on. Still, there were times when she would remember—like today with Jenny.

She stopped and glanced up across the yard to the shade of the scrub oak where Jenny Wyatt still sat. They seemed to have hit it off pretty well, she and Jenny. But maybe that wasn't so surprising. After all, they were a little like two pieces in the same puzzle:

Jenny, a child without a mother, and she, a mother without a child.

Casey turned and reached into her pocket for another nail, pounding it smoothly into the raw wood with a few powerful strokes. Of course, maybe someday she would have her own child. The doctors hadn't said it couldn't happen, just that it might be difficult. And she was only thirty-three. She still had a few childbearing years left ahead of her. The ticking of her biological clock seemed to grow louder and louder with each passing year. Maybe she would meet someone again—but that was a big maybe when she worked sixty hours a week and barely had enough time to sleep, let alone develop a social life.

Well, *maybe* she would, and *maybe* there would be time for dreams to come true and miracles to happen. But not now—not until she could be sure the danger was over and Bobby was strong enough to handle things on his own. Until then, there was too much to be done, too many people depending on her, too much riding on her shoulders.

Casey straightened up, glancing back just in time to see Jenny skip down the drive, swinging her lunch pail wildly back and forth as she went. A strange sort of tightness constricted her heart, and she felt her eyes begin to sting. She suddenly thought of Colton Wyatt and the cool suspicion she'd seen in his eyes. What made him so skeptical, and why didn't he trust her? She didn't want anything from him. Just this job, and maybe a little of his daughter's time.

* * *

"I wouldn't worry."

Colt picked up a small piece of carrot from the plastic bag in his hand and offered it to Mountain Lady. "You don't think so?"

Elias Milton shook his graying head as he reached for the towel from the rack beside the sink and thoroughly dried his hands. "She's doing fine. I don't know what Mac's talking about. I wouldn't expect her to foal early. She's still got a couple months to go."

Colt patted the forehead of the speckled Appaloosa mare and led her back into the stall. "He was just uneasy—thought she'd been restless, off her feed."

Elias snorted, repacking his oversize leather bag and firmly snapping it shut. "Do me a favor and tell that old coot of a stable hand of yours to stick to mucking stalls and leave the doctoring to me, okay?"

"Oh, sure, and why don't I just hop in a cage with an angry polecat while I'm at it?" Colt joked dryly, and they both laughed.

Colt knew better than most that MacKenzie Henderson was an old coot, and at seventy-three he was about as ornery and temperamental as they came. But he also knew he couldn't run things around the stables without him. Mac had worked for the previous owners of Cache Creek and just sort of came with the deal when Colt bought the place fifteen years ago. He not only mucked stalls and pitched hay, he knew just about everything there was to know about Appaloosas.

"By the way," Elias said as he grabbed his jacket from the tack hook along the stable wall. "How was the conference? Anything interesting going on?"

Colt shrugged, giving Mountain Lady a pat on the rear. "About the same. I ran into an old friend of yours, though."

"Friend of mine? You're kidding. Who?"

Colt reached into his back pocket and pulled out his wallet. After searching through it for a moment, he pulled out a business card and read from it. "Roger Scranton," he said, looking back at Elias. "From Chula Vista?"

"Well I'll be damned," Elias said, taking the card Colt offered him. "Roger Scranton. I don't think I've heard from him since veterinary school."

"That's what he said." Colt pulled the stall door closed and carefully secured the latch. "He asked me to send you his best."

"Chula Vista," Elias mused, reading off the card. "What the hell do you suppose he's doing down there?"

Colt shrugged. "Can't help you with that. We really didn't talk or anything. He'd just spotted San Andreas on my name tag and asked me if I knew you."

"Small world I tell you," Elias said with a sigh, tucking the card into the pocket of his shirt. He picked up his medical bag and followed Colt out of the stables and to his truck parked at the entrance. Tossing the bag onto the seat, he gestured up to the house with a nod. "Looks like you've got quite a project going on up there."

Colt glanced over his shoulder to the construction site. "Yeah, well, I'd promised Jenny."

"What are you adding—couple of bedrooms?"

Colt's gaze narrowed as he spotted the tall, slender silhouette of Casey Sullivan moving against the light. Even from a distance there was no mistaking her for a man, and he felt a tight knot in his stomach. "An office downstairs, two bedrooms upstairs."

Elias squinted, pointing to the logo on the vehicle parked in the drive. "What's that say on the side of the truck—Sullivan?"

Colt nodded. "Yeah, Sullivan Construction."

"Okay," Elias nodded. "I'm familiar with them."

"Oh, yeah?"

"Yeah, they did the reconstruction on the clinic last year. Damn good job, too." Elias slipped into the driver's seat and sighed. "Bobby Sullivan is one hell of a good guy. I'm glad to see things are working out for him again."

Colt's brow arched. "Again?"

"He had a tough time there a while back," Elias said, pausing for a moment and tapping his chin thoughtfully. "I can't remember the details exactly, but there was a traffic accident—either he hit someone or got hit." He shrugged, giving his head a shake. "Anyway, he lost his wife and young son. Took it pretty hard, too, as I remember. Sort of bottomed out, if you know what I mean." He raised his hand to mimic a drinking motion. "Hit the bottle pretty hard.

Would have lost the business, too, if it wasn't for Casey."

Colt stopped suddenly. "Casey?"

"Bobby's sister. You met her yet?"

"Yeah," Colt mumbled, nodding his head. "Yeah, I've met her."

Elias pursed his lips for a silent whistle and gave Colt a deliberate look. "She's something else, isn't she?" He wiggled his eyebrows wickedly, and his voice dropped an octave. "Sort of gives the word *construction* a whole knew meaning, if you get my drift. I have to admit, I wouldn't mind having her do a little work for me."

Colt scowled, ignoring Elias's low chuckle and licentious grin. He didn't exactly feel the need to defend Casey Sullivan's virtue, but for some reason he found Elias's remarks offensive and distasteful.

"But when it comes to construction, I guess she knows what the hell she's doing," Elias said, reaching for the ignition and bringing the engine to life. "I remember their old man, Buck. He built about half of San Andreas before he died. Bobby's good, I can tell you that, but Casey—she's the one who's the real chip off the old block. I guess it's not surprising that she's the pants of the operation now."

Colt looked at him. "What do you mean, the pants of the operation?"

Elias shrugged. "You know—in charge, runs things."

"Casey does?"

"Yeah," Elias said simply. "Bobby would be the first to tell you that. He runs the office, draws up plans, gives estimates, things like that. But Casey's the one who oversees everything—makes sure the jobs get done." He stopped for a moment, his grin widening, and motioned for Colt to lean close. "You know, it wouldn't be half bad having a woman wear the pants in the family if she filled them out as good as Casey Sullivan does."

Colt's frown deepened as he stepped back and watched Elias's truck speed along the drive and disappear down the road. He remembered all too well how Casey Sullivan looked in a pair of tight-fitting jeans. He hadn't needed Elias's lecherous remark or lame humor to bring that particular image to mind.

He slowly turned around, letting his gaze drift back toward the house and the construction going on in the distance. In fact, he hadn't needed any help in thinking of Casey Sullivan at all. He'd found himself thinking of her soft eyes and shapely bottom all morning.

He spotted her again, moving through the stacks of lumber and building supplies. He stopped, watching her slender form move against the sun—smooth, fluid motions that flowed easily and effortlessly.

He thought back to the exchange they'd had earlier in the driveway, remembering his shock and surprise when he realized the mistake he had made. He'd been so stunned, been so completely taken aback he'd been unable to do little more than stand there and stare. He'd felt like such an idiot and had a pretty good idea he'd acted like one, too. It was that, as much as his concern for Mountain Lady, that had him arranging things so that he would miss Jenny's picnic lunch. He'd had enough of the woman for one day.

Woman. He lifted an arm across his forehead, swiping at the sweat that had formed along his brow. She might not be the hulking male pervert he'd imagined her to be, but that didn't mean she still didn't pose a threat. She was a woman all right, and that had sent a new kind of red flag flying in his brain.

Like it or not, Casey Sullivan had made one hell of an impression on Jenny, and that made him uncomfortable—very uncomfortable. When it came to his daughter, he didn't trust any woman. Karen might have been the first woman to use Jenny to make him do what she wanted, but she hadn't been the only one.

Colt turned and headed back into the stables. Grabbing a brush from a hook on the wall, he reopened the door to Mountain Lady's stall.

"Easy, Lady," he said in a low, soothing voice as he slowly began to brush her. "Easy girl. Just relax. Relax, and let me take care of you."

Colt ran the brush over the mare's lean, muscular back, picturing the lean, slender silhouette of Casey Sullivan again in his mind. Maybe there would come a time when he wouldn't feel so suspicious, when he wouldn't feel so vulnerable when it came to Jenny. But not now. Now he remained on his guard, now he would keep a watchful eye open for women who offered friendship to his little girl, but wanted something more in return.

Holly had wanted to be Jenny's friend, too. Teaching preschool, Holly gave all her little students time and attention, but there was no doubting she'd taken a special interest in Jenny. Colt wouldn't deny he'd been grateful. Karen had just died, and Jenny missed her mother very much. Having the special attention of the teacher she adored had been a thrill.

When Holly first began showing up at the ranch unannounced, Colt had merely appreciated the extra time she'd been willing to give them. He hadn't been looking for hidden meanings or ulterior motives. He'd just been grateful for her help. It wasn't until she began talking about his *duty* to his daughter, his *obligation* to give the child the mother she wanted that it all began to sink in. When he'd made it clear to Holly he wasn't interested in marrying again—ever—her interest in Jenny came to an abrupt halt.

Colt finished brushing down Mountain Lady. He walked out of the stables and stared up at the house. He'd do just about anything for his daughter, but he'd already endured a loveless marriage once. Nothing was going to make him do it again.

Just then he saw Jenny run down the drive to meet Casey Sullivan. He watched as they talked and laughed together. What was it Casey Sullivan wanted, and how far was she willing to go to get it?

Chapter Three

"Jenny said she got this from you."

Casey jumped violently at the sound of the deep male voice so close behind her. Whirling around, she stared up into Colt Wyatt's angry eyes. "M-Mr. Wyatt, hello," she stammered, laughing nervously. "My goodness, you gave me quite a start."

Colt told himself he wasn't sorry, that he didn't regret having taken her by surprise, having thrown her off balance. As far as he was concerned, he'd had a damn good reason. He was furious, and she had some explaining to do.

"I found this in Jenny's lunch box," he said in a tight voice, trying hard not to notice how the color of her eyes matched the color of her hair almost exactly. "She said you gave it to her."

The anger in his voice surprised her more than his sneaking up behind her did. Casey stared down at the empty cupcake wrapper and blinked, giving her head a nod. "Uh, yes. Yes, I did." She looked back up at him. "Is there a problem?"

Colt crumbled the cellophane paper. "Yes, there's a problem. There's a problem because I don't like Jenny eating crap like this. I don't like having junk food in the house, and I don't like my daughter eating it, either. I've tried very hard to instill good eating habits in her, and I don't appreciate it when strangers undermine those efforts behind my back."

Casey blinked again, in a vain hope that the hapless gesture would somehow enable her to better believe what she was hearing. Was he serious? Could he possibly be this upset over a... a *cupcake?* She and Jenny had been exchanging things from their lunches all week—fruit, chips, Emma's homemade cookies—it never had occurred to her he would object.

Casey glanced back down at the crumpled wrapper in his hand, remembering Jenny's delight as she bit into the gooey cake. Was that why the little girl had relished the treat so much, because she'd never had anything like it before?

"Look, Mr. Wyatt," she said after a moment. "If I did something to upset you, I'm sorry. Believe me it wasn't intentional. I mean, Jenny didn't say anything, and I guess I just didn't think—"

"You're right," Colt said coolly, cutting her off. "You didn't think, and I'd appreciate it if in the future you would keep this—" he held the wrapper under her nose and gave it an angry shake "—and anything else like it to yourself and away from my daughter.''

Casey figured she must be in shock—she had to be. How else could she explain why she just stood there and watched him stalk off across the drive and down the walk toward the porch without so much as a word to defend herself?

The man was unbelievable. He'd not only been insulting, he'd been downright condescending and rude. He'd taken an innocent gesture and blown it all out of proportion. Maybe she had made a mistake by not getting his permission first before offering Jenny the cupcakes, but he was acting as though she'd hatched an evil scheme to usurp his authority with his daughter and lure her away. What was this guy's problem, anyway? Was he just suspicious by nature, or was there something about her that had him believing the worst?

He was about to climb the steps up the porch when feeling finally found its way back into her system, and she felt the anger, hot and potent. With a low groan she took off across the yard. If he thought he'd heard the end of this, he was mistaken.

''*Wyatt.*''

Colt stopped, but he wasn't entirely sure who had called out to him, until he turned around and saw her storming across the lawn. There had been such anger in the voice, such force and volume—he wouldn't have thought someone her size capable of such a thunderous outburst.

''You wanted something?''

"Yeah, I wanted something," Casey said, marching up to him until they were practically nose to nose. She planted her hands firmly on her hips and stared up into his cold, blue eyes. "I want to get straight on something. I want to know what it is I've done that's got you in such a snit?"

"Excuse me?" Colt asked deliberately, his blue eyes widening with surprise and indignity. "A . . . snit?"

"Yes, a *snit,*" she contended. "Now I figure you don't know me well enough to dislike me, and you haven't had time to find fault with the work I'm doing. So why don't you just save us both a lot of time and lay the cards on the table. Just say straight out what it is about me that bugs you so much?"

Colt's eyes darkened, and he felt the heavy pounding of his heart in his ears and at his throat. "I don't know what you're talking about."

"No? I'm talking about making mountains out of molehills. I'm talking about grasping at straws." She reached out and snatched the cellophane wrapper out of his hand, holding it between them. "I'm talking about pulling rabbits out of your hat just looking for an excuse to get upset."

Colt stared down at her, telling himself the rush of heat pulsating through his system was merely a result of anger. That it had nothing to do with the way her breasts rose and fell with emotion, straining against the soft blue of her chambray work shirt with each agitated breath.

"I hardly think expressing concern for your child could be considered grasping at straws," he said after a moment, grabbing the wrapper back and tossing it angrily to the ground. "And I don't need an excuse to protect my daughter."

"Is that what you call it, protecting Jenny?" She took a step closer. "From a cupcake, or from me?"

Colt cursed under his breath. What was the matter with him? Why hadn't he just left well enough alone instead of storming out here half-cocked like an angry stallion with a burr under its saddle? She was right—it was just a lousy cupcake—and yet he'd practically made a federal case out of it. What was the matter with him? Why was he trying so hard to be angry with her?

Because she'd been right about that, too. This whole thing hadn't been about cupcakes—it had to do with him and the fact that he hadn't been able to stop thinking about her. He'd wanted to confront her, had wanted an excuse to light into her and give her a piece of his mind. He had been angry all right—but not at her. At himself.

"Uh, look," he stammered after a moment. "Maybe I...maybe I did come on a little strong about—"

"It's because I'm a woman, isn't it?"

Colt stopped short, her sudden accusation throwing him for a moment. "What? What are you talking about?"

"This. All this," she said, gesturing wildly with her hands. "The job—the work. It's man's work, and you don't think I can do it because I'm a woman."

Colt's jaw dropped. He had to admit discovering a woman construction worker had been a bit of a surprise, but it had never occurred to him to question whether she could do the job or not. Everything about her seemed to radiate confidence and competence, and he didn't doubt she could do anything she set her mind to.

"No," he said, giving his head a small shake. "Look, you being a woman has nothing to do—"

"Well, let me tell you something, Mr. Colton Wyatt," Casey continued, cutting him off. "You're not the first Neanderthal I've run into, and I'm sure you won't be the last."

"Look, Miss Sullivan—"

"This is the twentieth century, not the Dark Ages, and let me tell you," Casey stormed on, giving him no time to finish. "You won't find a man in this community—in this state—who knows more about construction than I do."

"I don't doubt it, if you'll just listen—"

But she wouldn't. Instead, she exploded into a fury of righteous indignation. "And I dare you," she said through gritted teeth, ramming a finger into his chest, "to find anyone—*anyone,* man or woman—who can do the work I do. And I mean good work, top-notch..."

"Miss Sullivan—" Colt tried again.

"...not this slipshod junk you get from a lot of these outfits, I'm talking first-rate work..."

"If you'd just give me a chance," Colt said, talking over her. "Miss Sullivan, just listen—"

"...You try and find someone who can do the job better than me. Just try. Try and find someone who can give you the quality work I can give you in the shortest time possible—"

In desperation, Colt drew in a deep breath and reached for her. *"Casey!"*

Casey's diatribe came to an abrupt halt, and her eyes grew wide. He'd never called her by her first name before, and hearing him say it now brought her up short. She looked up at him, her heart pounding and her chest moving with quick, excited breaths. It was only then that she realized he was holding her—one strong hand planted firmly around each of her upper arms.

"Wh-wh—" She stopped when her voice failed, and cleared her throat loudly. "What is it?"

"Slow down," he said quietly and deliberately, the hands on her arms tightening slightly. "Give me a chance to explain."

Casey took a deep breath, feeling the heat from his hands seep through the fabric of her shirt. She felt foolish now for having gone on so. Why should she care what he thought of her? He'd hired her to do a job, nothing more—it wasn't necessary that they get along. After all, they didn't have to be friends, they didn't even have to like each other.

"Explain what?" she asked, moving back a step and carefully pulling herself free of his hold. She felt better now that he wasn't touching her, but the wariness continued. So it was more defense than defiance that had her taking another step backwards and had her folding her arms protectively across her chest.

Colt looked down into her dusky brown eyes. For some ridiculous reason, he suddenly felt like smiling. But the expression on her face told him she was hardly in the mood for humor. "That you've got it all wrong."

"Is that a fact?"

"Yes, it is," he said, his voice softening. "Despite what you may think, or what it might have sounded like to you, I'm not stuck in the Dark Ages and I don't think because you're a woman you can't swing a hammer or saw a piece of wood."

"No?"

"No," he said simply.

Casey's gaze narrowed, and she gave him a skeptical look. "Then what is your problem, Mr. Wyatt?"

"My problem, Miss Sullivan," Colt said, taking a step closer. "Is that I can be kind of a jerk sometimes—especially where my daughter is concerned. I came on too strong before. I admit it, and...and I apologize."

Casey stared up at him, almost as surprised by this confession as she'd been by his outburst in the first place. He had acted like a jerk, but at least he was willing to admit it. And maybe, just maybe, she'd come on a little strong herself.

"Well," she said with a small shrug, shifting her weight. "Maybe we both got off on the wrong foot."

Colt watched as the delicate lines around her mouth and eyes softened and disappeared, thinking how much younger and prettier she looked when she wasn't reading him the riot act. But then...as he thought about it, she hadn't looked all that bad when she'd been raging at him, either.

Slowly he extended his hand out to her. "How about we try and forget this and start all over?"

Casey stared down at his outstretched hand wondering whether she should take it or not. The man had been unbelievably rude to her, but he was a paying customer and for that reason alone she should swallow her pride and make amends. And there was Jenny to consider, as well. She was a smart little girl, and no doubt it wouldn't take her long to pick up on any tension between them.

Still, Casey found herself hesitating. Colt Wyatt made her nervous. She felt uneasy around him—uneasy and strangely vulnerable. She thought of how it had felt to have his hands on her, thought about the heat that had swamped her system and the images that had begun to fill her mind. Just thinking about it now had a shiver of sensation running the length of her spine. She had felt warmth from those hands, strength and power.

Casey had never been intimidated by a man's strength. She was used to being around men—big men, strong men—men who worked with their hands and used their physical strength. But the power she had felt in Colt's hands had been very, very different. It bothered her, disturbed her and made her feel vulnerable. It was what had her holding back and made her reluctant to touch him again.

"I won't bite," he said after a moment. "Not again, anyway."

Casey heard the humor in his voice and felt the color rise in her cheeks. "Is that a promise?" she asked dryly as she slipped her hand into his.

"I never lie," he said, closing his fingers around her slender ones. "Not to women who operate heavy equipment, anyway."

Casey watched the hard lines of his mouth soften almost to a smile and felt the steady rhythm of her heart falter and skip a few beats. Maybe Colton Wyatt wouldn't bite, but he was a danger all the same.

"I don't operate heavy equipment," she told him pointedly. "But I never go anywhere without my nail gun."

"What is it?"

Casey smiled, watching Jenny's eyes grow wide with excitement and thinking how much she looked like Colt. The resemblance was unmistakable. They shared the same high cheekbones, the same slender nose, the same brilliant blue eyes. Except Jenny's eyes were warm and trusting when they looked at her. Colt's were still filled with apprehension and doubt.

"Why don't you open it up and find out?" Casey suggested, handing Jenny the package wrapped in sturdy brown paper with a rustic-looking straw bow on the top.

Jenny tore through the heavy paper and yanked open the cover of the small, flat box inside. "A tool belt," she shrieked, lifting it up out of the box. "With real tools and everything—just like yours." Spontaneously, she turned and threw her arms around Casey's neck, squeezing tight. "Oh, thank you, Casey. Thank you."

Jenny's impetuous bear hug had been a surprise, which made it all the more endearing. It had been such a genuine reaction, so honest and real, Casey found herself responding with too much emotion.

"Well, I figure if you're going to be part of the crew," she said quickly, blinking away the stinging sensation in her eyes. "It's time you started looking like one."

"And they're real, too," Jenny said, pulling back and slipping the belt around her waist. "Really...*real*—not toys."

"Well, they're a little smaller than most," Casey said, explaining about the scaled-down hammer, screwdrivers and work gloves that dangled through the leather loops of the belt. "But you're right about them not being toys." She reached down and helped Jenny thread the end through the buckle. "They're real, and it's important that you learn to use them correctly. There," she said, once the buckle was secured tight. "Step back and let's see how that looks."

Jenny marched back several paces and struck a pose. "Just like you," she giggled, abruptly bending in the middle to get a better look herself.

"Not quite," Casey said, reaching for the door of her truck. Pulling it open, she leaned across the seat. "The most important thing a construction worker learns is to properly protect themselves on a job site."

Once again Jenny's eyes grew like saucers when she saw what Casey held in her hand. "A hard hat? For me? Oh, Casey, is it really for me?"

"For you," Casey repeated, feeling the emotion grow thick in her throat once again. The sting in her eyes was back, and she blinked fiercely to prevent tears from forming.

She still remembered the day Buck had brought that hat home for her. She'd been about Jenny's age then, and had felt very grown-up and important wearing a hat just like her dad's. It had been one of the best gifts she could ever remember getting, and it had been a precious keepsake all these years.

And of course, she'd always assumed that one day she would give it to her own little girl . . . only the likelihood of that ever happening seemed remote, if not impossible now. When she'd walked into her office the other day and spotted the little hat looking dusty and abandoned on the top of a bookcase, she'd decided it had been on the shelf long enough. She'd taken it down and cleaned it up. It was time to put it to good use again.

Casey slipped the hard hat down over Jenny's soft little ringlets and took a step back. Jenny might not be her daughter, but she saw a lot of herself in the little girl just the same. Like Jenny, she once had dreamed big dreams, once had an imagination that knew no limits, and a compassion that recognized no bounds—and for some reason, passing the hat on to her just somehow felt right.

"Wow," Jenny said breathlessly, running a hand along the top of her head. "A real hard hat."

Casey smiled, thinking how adorable she looked with her big, blue eyes shining and her golden curls tumbling out from beneath the bright yellow hat. "Well, you're officially part of the crew now," she said, slamming the door of her truck and reaching for her own tool belt from the back. Strapping it on, she held out a hand to Jenny. "Ready to get to work?"

"Honest?" Jenny gasped, staring up with wide, expectant eyes. "You mean it? I can really help?"

Casey smiled. "Hey, I need all the good workers I can get."

Jenny smiled up at her, slipping her tiny hand into Casey's. "Okay."

Colt felt the breath catch in his throat, causing a momentary strangling sensation, and he coughed out loud. He came to such an abrupt halt that Mountain Lady collided into him, and the contact jarred them both.

"Easy girl," he mumbled absently, when she reared her head back and strained against the rein in his hands. "Easy."

He could do little else to calm the prize mare down. He was too distracted, too flabbergasted by the sight in front of him to do anything more than stand and stare. There, walking along the drive toward the construction site, was Casey, hand in hand with Jenny. Only that in itself wasn't particularly unusual. Over the course of the past three weeks he'd almost become accustomed to seeing the two of them together.

What had him standing there unable to move or think was the sight of Jenny—*his* Jenny—his very own little girl marching down the driveway wearing a tool belt and hard hat, and looking very much like a pint-size carbon copy of Casey.

Mountain Lady nudged against his arm and stamped her foot restlessly. She wanted to return to her stall and the bag of fresh oats she knew would be waiting there. But Colt ignored the mare's fidgeting. He couldn't seem to take his eyes off Jenny and Casey.

He wasn't sure how he felt seeing the two of them together like that. As the days had turned into weeks, and progress on the new wing of the house began to take shape, he was used to hearing Jenny's nightly routine of "Casey said this," and "Casey said that." It had almost become as much a part of their nightly ritual as reading a bedtime story and checking under the bed for the boogeyman.

And while he had to admit Jenny's fascination with Casey still made him uneasy, he'd done his best to keep those feelings to himself. After all, it was just a temporary thing. In another month or so, construction on the house would be finished. Hopefully she would be too busy, too caught up in the excitement of moving into her new bedroom and getting ready to start kindergarten to notice that Casey Sullivan had slipped out of her life for good.

Colt reached up and gave Mountain Lady a reassuring pat on the nose, watching as Casey carefully rested a small piece of lumber securely across the top of two sturdier pieces and helped Jenny hammer a nail straight into the middle of it.

She was very patient, he had to give her that, and he appreciated how Casey stressed the importance of safety and taking the proper precautions, but still he couldn't help feeling uncomfortable. What precautions could he take to protect Jenny from getting hurt again?

Jenny hammered down several more nails, and Casey hovered close by, keeping a watchful eye on her progress. The two of them made quite a pair—dressed alike with their tool belts and hard hats. He almost felt as though he were watching a mother with her child— except Casey Sullivan had no children, and Jenny belonged to him. Still, watching them, he felt a strange mixture of compassion and contention brewing in his gut.

Casey bent close to inspect Jenny's progress, and the morning sun glinted brightly off her hat. It had been three weeks since that fiasco with the cupcake wrapper, and yet he still cringed when he thought of it. Things had been strained since then, and what few words they'd exchanged had centered strictly on business. He admitted he'd done his best to steer clear of her in the faint hope she'd just forget the whole unpleasant thing, but it was obvious she hadn't forgotten a thing.

She hadn't taken any chances this time. She'd found him late yesterday afternoon and asked if he would have any objections to her giving Jenny "a few tools" to keep as her own. It was obvious she didn't want another misunderstanding, and took careful pains to assure him she would instruct Jenny on the proper use and the proper care of the tools.

She'd been diplomatic enough, but he'd felt stupid, anyway. She no doubt saw him as a hysterical parent and wanted to avoid doing anything that might "set him off" again. He'd given his permission as much to show her he wasn't a complete ogre as it was in response to her generous offer.

Just then Jenny stood up and slipped the small handle of the hammer through the loop on her belt. Of course, he hadn't imagined the "few tools" Casey had referred to would be anything like this, and it only made him feel all the more foolish for having been such a jerk before.

"Damn fool thing if you ask me."

Colt turned and looked at MacKenzie Henderson, who stood gazing up the hill beside him. His stubbled beard looked grizzled and gray, and his faded brown eyes had narrowed to slits.

"What's that, Mac?"

The old man shook his head, reaching out and taking the reins of Mountain Lady. "A woman in a hard hat and wearing a tool belt. It's not natural I tell you. That young woman needs a man and a couple of kids to look after, not be hammering nails and ordering men around." He turned and pulled on the reins, leading Mountain Lady down the path toward the stables. "Don't know what this world's coming to." He stopped after a few steps and turned around. "And if that were my daughter up there, you can be damn sure I'd be putting a stop to that kind of business." He shook his head once more and started down the path again. "No, siree, I don't know what this world's coming to—women using hammers."

Colt smiled as he watched Mac make his way toward the stable with Mountain Lady dutifully following alongside. But he remembered Casey's tirade about that sort of "Neanderthal" thinking and wondered what her reaction to Mac would have been.

"Daddy!" Jenny shrieked when she spotted him from across the yard. She ran down the slope toward the stables, the tools on her belt swinging wildly with every move. "Daddy, look, see what Casey gave me."

Colt smiled and gave his daughter a wave. "Hey, what's this?" he called out, walking up the slope toward her. "Do we have a new worker around here?"

Jenny giggled when she reached her father, proudly displaying the tool belt. "It's just like hers, just like Casey's."

"I'll say it is," he said, kneeling down and making a dramatic play of inspecting the belt.

"I've got a hammer and a screwdriver," she said, pointing everything out. "And another screwdriver, and work gloves, too."

"You sure do," he said, seeing the look of delight on her face and feeling his heart swell in his chest. "You can get a lot done with a set like this. You going to let me borrow them sometime?"

Jenny's grin widened, and she gave him a playful swat on the shoulder. "Oh, Daddy, you're so silly." She made a small fist, giving the hat on her head a tap. "And did you see this, too? It's a hard hat, Daddy— a real hard hat. You can hit me on the head and it won't even hurt."

"I can see that," Colt said, giving it a tap himself. "Just your size, too."

"Casey says I'm one of the crew now," Jenny told him, her face growing serious. "*Officially*—just like Jake and Ronnie."

"Officially you say," he mused, pulling his daughter close for a hug just as Casey made her way down the slope to where they stood. He looked up at her, rising slowly to his feet. "I hope Jenny thanked you."

"Oh, she did," Casey assured him, giving Jenny a wink and remembering the ridiculously strong burst of emotion she'd felt from Jenny's spontaneous hug.

"We hammered nails," Jenny announced proudly, giving the leg of her father's jeans a tug and pointing up the slope. "And Casey let me do it all by myself."

Colt glanced down at Jenny, then back to Casey's smoky brown eyes. "This was really nice of you."

Casey gave her head a small shake. "I enjoyed it. I'm biased, but tools shouldn't just be for boys. I think every little girl should have her own and know how to use them."

"No dolls?" he asked dryly.

"Oh, dolls are okay, too," she admitted. "But why should boys have all the fun?"

Chapter Four

"Do you have a few minutes?"

Colt, intent on enjoying his morning coffee and newspaper on the front porch swing, was surprised to find Casey standing on the front walk looking up at him. She was dressed in her standard work clothes, but there was no hard hat now, no tool belt dangling from her waist, and her long hair tumbled thick and unchecked down her back. It was barely past six, the sun had hardly risen from the horizon, and he hadn't expected to see her, or any of the crew, for at least another hour or so.

"Sure," he said, waving her up the porch steps. He leaned forward, setting his coffee mug on the table beside the swing, and carefully folded the paper. "I didn't hear you drive up."

"I, uh, I parked around back," she mumbled, hesitating for a minute. With his nose in a newspaper, she hadn't realized he wasn't wearing a shirt, and the sight of him sitting there bare-chested was a little unnerving. Embarrassed, she fumbled with the long tube she carried, banging it loudly against the iron railing as she climbed the steps to the porch. The hard soles of her work boots sounded loud when she walked on the rustic terra-cotta tile of the porch, and only made her more aware of the fact that he watched her every move. "I didn't want to disturb anyone in the house."

"You're early this morning," he said, wishing now he'd tossed a T-shirt on over his jeans. "Is there a problem?"

"No, no, nothing like that," she assured him, shaking her head. "I'd just been turning this idea around in my head for a while." She lifted the tube up. "I thought I'd come by early and check some things out."

"Coffee?" he asked, pointing to the insulated pot beside his mug.

Casey shook her head again, trying desperately to keep herself from looking directly at his chest. "No, thanks, I've got a thermos in the truck."

"So, what's this idea you've had?" he asked, picking up the newspaper from beside him on the swing and tossing it aside. "Here, sit down."

Casey hesitated again, staring at the empty space on the swing beside him as though it were wired with electricity. Why hadn't she waited a little longer? She'd practically gotten him out of bed, and the thought of him and that chest and those cool blue eyes in a bed made her feel all the more awkward and uncomfortable. How was she supposed to talk business with him dressed—or rather *undressed*—like that?

"I know you went over all this with Bobby," she said, flipping the cap off the tube and sliding out a long, neatly rolled length of paper. She lowered herself gingerly onto the porch swing beside him. "But I had some questions about this area here, in your office." She unrolled the blueprint and indicated a spot on the plans. "It's marked storage. Bobby's indicated in my notes that you talked about a walk-in type of thing?"

Colt bent close, studying the blueprint. The side of his leg made contact with hers, and heat immediately began to radiate through his body. "To be honest, I don't really remember."

She shifted uneasily, trying to ignore the heat from his leg that was now spreading through her bloodstream. "So you didn't have something in mind for this space? I mean, something specific?"

He looked down at the plans again. "Not really— just a place to keep the boxes of breeding records, information on the ranch—things like that," he said, turning to her. "Why?"

He listened as she launched into a detailed explanation, looking closely at the places she indicated on the blueprint, and nodding along when she made a point. It wasn't that he couldn't hear her, because he could—every word. He just couldn't seem to make the words register in his brain. He'd become too caught up in the soft curve of her neck, too distracted by the way she caught her bottom lip between her teeth whenever she paused to think. He became sidetracked every time she impatiently pushed her hair back from her face—because each time she did, it would release a soft fragrance that swirled about him like a cloud, making him light-headed and dizzy with its delicate scent. His mind wandered, and he couldn't stop sultry, forbidden images from filling his brain.

What would it be like to touch such exquisite skin, to run his lips along the lush curves of her neck and pull that full lower lip between his own teeth? What would it be like to hold her, to feel that strong, lean body beneath him, to pull her into his arms for an embrace and lose himself in the heady fragrance of flowers and sunshine from her long, silky hair?

"See what I mean?"

It took him a minute to realize she had stopped talking and was looking at him with wide, expectant eyes. He could only imagine what a picture he made, sitting there staring at her with a blank expression—dazed and lost in thought. She already thought he was a jerk, now she was going to think him an idiot—especially since he didn't have a clue as to what she'd been talking about.

"I'm . . . I'm sorry," he stammered, feeling embarrassed and confused. He thought again of the seductive images that had filled his mind, and his body flushed hot. "What was that?"

"Well, just keep in mind I'm not talking about any major structural changes," she carefully emphasized, taking his questions as normal confusion. "I'm talking about leaving this back wall just as it is here in the blueprints. All we're talking about changing would be this section here—for the shelving. I know where I could pick up some oak for you at a very reasonable cost. It would make a beautiful bookcase. And as you can see, it would still leave you with a considerable space along this back section for storage."

"A bookcase," he repeated, desperate to piece together the gist of what she'd been saying. "Here?"

Casey nodded, her teeth clenched tightly together. Was he being obtuse just to annoy her? Despite his attempt to "start over," she couldn't forget the man had had something against her at first. She should have known he wouldn't be open to an idea from her—even if it was a good one and might end up saving him some money. Why had she even bothered?

"Look, it was just a suggestion," she said tersely, reaching for the end of the blueprint and starting to roll it up again. "I just thought with this being an office, most people would find the shelf space preferable. But if you'd rather not..."

"No," he said, stopping her from rolling the blueprint any further with a hand on hers. Something in the back of his brain had registered that her skin felt smooth and soft and warm. "No, look, I'm sorry. I... I have a little trouble getting anything to sink in before my full dose of caffeine in the morning. Could you maybe run that by me again?"

Casey felt his hard palm against the top of her hand and froze. What she needed at the moment was a little distance between them—not have him touching her. She was altogether too aware of him as it was, already having a difficult time trying not to notice how hard and strong his arms were, or how light and golden the hair along his chest looked against his smooth, tanned skin. She didn't need the added distraction of his hand on hers.

"If you want," she murmured, slipping her hand free and rolling out the blueprint again.

This time Colt listened intently, visualizing the space and the bookshelves she was suggesting. He remembered that when Bob Sullivan had suggested a storage area adjacent to the office, he had liked the idea. But it was obvious now that Casey's plan would make better use of the space. He liked the idea of a built-in bookcase for his office and imagined it stacked with his books and plaques and photographs.

Colt couldn't help thinking back to what Elias had said about Casey being in charge of the business. How did that happen? Did she have a better feel for things than her brother? Was she just a "chip off the old block," following in her father's footsteps, or was there something more to it?

Colt looked up from the plans, watching as she once again pushed her hair back from her face, and catching a faint whiff of its sweet, clean fragrance. It would have been very easy to let his mind wander further, to allow it to drift back to that heady place of image and sensation, but he kept himself in check. He'd embarrassed himself once by not paying attention to what she said, he couldn't afford to do it again. Still he watched, and he wondered.

Elias had also mentioned something about a drinking problem Bob once had. Was that why Casey was now the "pants" of the operation? Was that what had caused a big brother to be taking orders from his little sister?

Colt turned these things over in the back of his mind as he listened to her describe the pros and cons of oiled finishes versus urethane varnish on oak shelving, trying to decide what it was about her that made him so interested. It was more than her beauty—although God knows that interested him more than he was comfortable with. A man would have to be dead not to have noticed those eyes, and that figure.

But it was more than that, and it was more than the fact that she was a woman working in a traditionally male-dominated field. He'd seen her with her crew, seen her issuing orders and shouting out commands. There wasn't a doubt in his mind that when it came to bosses, she was as tough and as exacting as they came. In the horse business, he knew women who "wore the pants," who took charge and did jobs traditionally thought of as men's work. So what was it about this particular woman that seemed to fascinate him so?

He thought of her with Jenny, of seeing the two of them together—laughing and talking. He thought of the way she looked at his daughter and the things she said; the tone of her voice and the natural, easy-going relationship the two of them shared.

Colt felt a tight, almost breathless sensation in his chest. Was that why he was so curious, why he couldn't seem to get the woman out of his mind and wanted to know everything about her? Was it the way she was with Jenny—that soft, maternal side she showed that seemed so diametrically opposed to the woman he'd watched working on the building site?

Which woman was she—Casey, the tough, able-bodied construction worker, or Cassandra, the soft, gentle earth mother?

"Basically, that's it," she said, sitting back and allowing him time to peruse the blueprint and absorb what she'd suggested. "Of course it's up to you—I'll build it however you want, but it's something to think about. I think it would look great."

She leaned back against the slats of the swing and waited. With his attention distracted by the plans, she allowed her gaze to drift over his strong arms and muscular back, feeling a deep flush begin to crawl up her neck and into her cheeks.

What was the matter with her? She was acting like she'd never seen a man's bare chest before, and yet she had—dozens of times. On hot days, the men on her work crews would often strip off their shirts. It was no big deal. A man's physique was certainly no mystery to her. She'd managed to look at them without getting all hot and bothered, without feeling flustered and embarrassed like some old maid schoolteacher sneaking a peak at the custodian.

But seeing Colt Wyatt without a shirt was something very different. It was a big deal. He wasn't one of her workers, wasn't one of the rough-and-tumble guys she would talk to and joke with on the job site. He was her client, her customer, and a certain protocol was in order. She had no business seeing him half-dressed, no business thinking what she was thinking.

And what she was thinking made her even more uncomfortable and the stain on her cheeks darken. Her life had always been filled with men—her dad,

Bobby, the men on the crew. Only there had been no one special in her life since Charlie—no one she had wanted or wanted to be with—which made it all the more ridiculous that she would choose to fantasize about Colt Wyatt.

The man didn't even particularly like her, had subtly made that clear to her on more than one occasion. And yet that didn't seem to stop her from thinking about what it would be like to have those strong arms around her, to have them pull her tight against his hard, flat stomach and hold her close.

She shifted uneasily, causing the swing to sway, and consequently his leg pressed even more tightly against hers. The movement sent a wave of heat traveling up her body, and she felt its wake in a flush of warmth at the collar of her shirt. She thought of the golden dusting of hair along his chest and wondered if his legs had the same covering. It had looked so soft against his tanned skin, and she wondered if she were to touch it, if it would feel the same way against...

"Do it and find out."

Casey jumped violently and drew in a breath so quickly she nearly strangled on it. "Wh-what?"

"The bookcase," Colt said, looking up from the plans and giving her a smile. "I think it would look great, too. Let's do it and find out."

"Oh, yes," she said, feeling the color in her face grow deeper. "Yes, we'll...we'll do it. That's great."

She just wanted to die, just wished the floor would open up and hide her away so she would never have to face him again. It didn't matter that he didn't know what it was she'd been thinking, that he had no way of knowing she'd been sitting there daydreaming about him. *She* knew, and that was bad enough.

Her cheeks flamed, and all she could think about was getting out of that swing and away from him as fast as she could. She forgot about the blueprint balanced on her lap, forgot about the long tube resting at her side. They no longer seemed important—until she moved to get up and sent them sliding to the floor.

"Oh, no," she groaned, staring down at the clutter at her feet.

"Here, let me," Colt said, leaning down and retrieving the things from the porch tiles. He stood up, slowly rolling the blueprint into a long cylinder and slipping it back into the tube. "It's a good idea—the bookcase, I mean. I appreciate the suggestion."

Casey kept her gaze fixed on the tube in his hand, not wanting to meet his eyes. "Just doing my job."

"No, I don't think so," he said simply, handing her the tube. "Doing your job would have been following the plans as they're drawn. This looks like duty above and beyond."

Casey slid the tube under her arm and started for the steps. She gave Jake a wave as he passed down the drive in his ratty old truck, ready to start work.

"Things always come up, on a job, that aren't in the plans," she told Colt, feeling better now that their bodies were no longer touching and her face had begun to cool. "You always find things you can improve on, or didn't think of before."

"Learn that from your dad?"

She stopped and turned back to him. "You knew my dad?"

"No, Bob mentioned him when we'd talked, that's all," Colt said, neglecting to add he'd heard the same thing from Elias Milton. "Said he'd known just about everything there was to know about the construction business."

Casey nodded. "Yeah, he did. Nobody was better than Buck."

"Not even you?"

She looked up at him and laughed. "Oh, I'm good, but I've still got a ways to go before I catch up with him."

"It must have pleased him to have both his children follow in his footsteps."

"I suppose," Casey said with a shrug, remembering the look on her father's face the day she'd lost her baby. It had been the only time she'd ever seen her father cry.

Colt watched the play of emotion on her face and wondered what it was she wasn't saying. "You miss him a lot, don't you?"

She nodded again, gazing off into the distance and spotting Ronnie's old station wagon along the road, and her smile grew wistful. "I do. Sometimes I can hardly believe it's been almost six years since he died."

"And your mom?"

"She died when I was just a baby. I never knew her," she said, reaching the walk and coming to a stop. "At least Jenny has memories of her mother—remembers her as a real person—not just a face in a picture."

Colt's expression stiffened. "I'm not so sure that's a good thing."

Casey gave him a curious look. "Oh?"

Colt hesitated. He wasn't in the habit of talking about his wife to anyone and wasn't sure why he was so willing to talk to Casey about her now. "Karen, Jenny's mother, wasn't a very happy person. She had a lot of problems, a lot of difficulties coping. She was never really able to give of herself the way a parent has to for their children." He paused, sinking his hands deep into his pockets and losing himself in thought. "There are things about her mother I hope Jenny doesn't remember, things I'd just as soon she forget. I worry about that sometimes."

Casey watched the pain cross his face and something stirred deep inside her. He was a complicated man—and had been a little hard on her. But she didn't doubt that he was a good man—strong and caring. She couldn't know what kind of husband he had been, but his devotion to Jenny was apparent, and that said a lot about him. Like all the men she'd known, he didn't like feeling weak, didn't like feeling exposed and vulnerable. Yet when it came to Jenny, he was not only vulnerable, his heart was wide open.

"It's tough growing up without a mother—believe me, I know," she said in a quiet voice. "But I also know what it means to have a father who loves you and cares about you and would give you the world if he could. As far as I'm concerned, that can make up for a lot." She stopped, forgetting for a moment that he was her employer, that he stood in the morning sun clad only in a pair of faded jeans. For the moment he was simply Jenny's dad—a father in dire need of support. Consciously or unconsciously, she wasn't sure, but somehow her hand wound up on his arm. "Relax, Colt, Jenny's a lucky little girl. She's going to be just fine."

Colt felt the blood in his veins spread a thick, heavy warmth through his system. Who was this woman, and what kind of strange power did she wield over him? She had him telling her things he'd never told another living soul—things about Jenny and Karen—about his fears and his concerns. And what was it about her softly spoken words of assurance that had given him such comfort and relieved so many fears?

Slipping her hand into his, he wove her long, smooth fingers through his. It had been a long time since he'd wanted a woman more than physically, but he was finding he wanted this one very much.

"Casey," he murmured in a voice made harsh with need and emotion. His hands found their way to her hips, and he pulled her close, so close he could see the faint flecks of gold in the brown of her eyes, could smell the subtle fragrance of her hair. "Casey."

"*Casey!*"

The moment shattered like a sheet of glass falling against the pavement. Jenny came racing through the screen door, flying across the porch and down the steps at record speed.

Casey turned at the sound of her name, feeling dazed and wooden as she watched Jenny run down the walk toward her. Everything felt so unreal, so imaginary, and nothing seemed to play out at normal speed. Her arms and legs felt heavy and stiff, and moving had become difficult, if not impossible. It was as though all this were happening in a dream somewhere and not to her at all.

Only it *was* happening to her. She stood there, practically in Colt Wyatt's arms, and she wasn't sure at the moment exactly how it had happened.

"Good morning, Jenny," she heard her voice call out, some kind of automatic reflex kicking in. "What are you doing up so early?"

Colt dropped his hold on Casey's hand and stepped to one side. He watched as she leaned down and greeted Jenny, wondering at her ability to react and respond. How could she do that? He was barely able to think.

He felt stupid standing there—his heart pulsing loudly in his ears and his entire system in an uproar. He needed time to pull himself together.

Since Karen had died, he'd been very careful who he'd allowed into his life. He'd steered clear of involvements and had been careful to avoid any entanglements. But not to protect himself... to protect Jenny.

And yet when he'd looked into Casey Sullivan's eyes just now, he seemed to forget about all those precautions and safeguards. The only thing on his mind at that moment had been Casey and what it would feel like to hold her in his arms.

Had he lost his mind? What if Jenny hadn't come out when she had, what would have happened then? Would he have taken the woman in his arms? Would he have pressed her to him tight?

Colt closed his eyes. He didn't even want to think what could have happened after that. He hardly knew the woman. He didn't know who she was or what she wanted. All he knew was that she'd managed to stir something in him that had lain dormant for a very long time, something that had him thinking of his own selfish needs and momentarily forgetting about protecting his daughter. It only proved to him just how really dangerous the woman was—and how important it was for him to stay as far away from her as possible.

He heard Jenny giggle and opened his eyes. She chattered to Casey, the lacy ruffles of her summer shortie pajamas fluttering about her little legs as she jumped about excitedly. She was talking about the Fourth of July celebration they had every year, when they invited friends and family, the MLHA's board members and their families to the ranch for a barbecue. It was coming up in another week, and Jenny's excitement was growing.

"And...and last year we had a fire in the fire ring and toasted marshmallows and made 's'mores.' All the little kids had to have their parents help them, but Daddy let me hold mine over the fire all by myself."

"All by yourself?" Casey asked, watching Jenny's blue eyes dance. "That's pretty good."

"Uh-huh," Jenny said, nodding her head and making her golden curls jiggle. "And I was only this many last summer." She stopped and held up four chubby fingers. "Only four. But this year we get to roast hot dogs over the fire. Daddy said, didn't you, Daddy?" She turned and flashed her father a smile, but didn't wait for a response. "Emma's got a *big* box of hot dogs." She stretched her arms out wide. "Like this."

"Sounds like she's planned enough for an army," Casey said with a laugh, reaching out and pushing one errant curl back from Jenny's clear brow. She listened while Jenny talked on about sack races and firework displays, but a pang of guilt had her heart feeling heavy.

Jenny was too young to pick up on any undercurrents of tension or to appreciate what an awkward scene she had walked in on. But what would have happened had she come flying through that door a few minutes later; what would her reaction have been then?

Inwardly Casey flinched. What had happened today had been a fluke, a momentary lapse in judgment, and she was going to have to make darn sure nothing like it ever happened again. This was a small community, and Bobby's drinking had already brought them their share of gossip and innuendo. She'd worked too hard and too long to rebuild the reputation of Sullivan Construction to throw it all away on an attraction she neither welcomed nor wanted.

Colt felt Jenny's impatient tug on his jeans and saw her anxious expression. He shot a nervous look in Casey's direction, something he'd been trying to avoid since Jenny had interrupted them.

"I'm sorry, sweetheart," he said, looking back at his daughter and kneeling down in front of her. He settled a big hand on either side of her tiny frame and focused his attention. "What was that you said?"

"Tell Casey," Jenny said, throwing her arms around his neck and giving him a kiss. "Tell Casey you want her to come to the barbecue, too."

Chapter Five

Colt lifted the heavy bag of charcoal off the wheelbarrow and rested it alongside the others near the oversize grill. Eight bags—that should just about do it, he thought. Jenny might be excited about roasting hot dogs over an open fire, but the forty or so others coming to the barbecue this afternoon were expecting something a little different, Colt knew.

He straightened up, swiping at the sweat along his brow, and glanced back at the three large coolers resting in the shade of one of the red, white and blue striped awnings that were stretched out across the lawn. The hundred pounds of baby back ribs that filled those coolers, marinating in his secret barbecue sauce, were what everyone had come to expect.

He stretched his back, wiping his brow again. It was hot, which wasn't unusual for the Fourth of July, and his work shirt was soaked with sweat. But that was okay. He was finished now. It was a big job, coordinating everything and putting together a dinner the size of this one, but he'd done it and couldn't help but feel pleased.

Smiling broadly, he looked out across the yard. The canopies were up, the picnic tables were in place, and the beer was on ice. He had only to light the charcoal, take a shower, and he'd be ready to greet his guests in less than an hour.

Guests. Colt's satisfied smile stiffened and slowly fell. That included Casey Sullivan.

He still wasn't sure exactly how it had happened. One minute he'd been standing there so embarrassed that he'd been telling himself he was going to do his best to stay away from the woman, and the next he'd been joining Jenny in convincing her to come to their holiday celebration. Just what was it going to take for him to swear off the woman?

He bent down and picked up the handles of the wheelbarrow, starting across the yard toward the toolshed. He didn't want her to come, didn't want her meeting his family and spending time with his friends. She worked for him, was simply someone he'd hired to do a job. There was nothing in the contract between them that said he had to socialize with her, as well.

As he walked into the shade of the house, he glanced up at the looming skeleton of the wing addition. It had been nearly four weeks since construction had started, and it was really beginning to take shape. With both the first and second stories fully framed, and most of the drywall up, it was easier to imagine just how the whole thing was going to look when it was completed.

Watching it take shape had been a real experience for Jenny, and he had to admit that as things progressed, he felt a bubble of anticipation himself. When completed, it would be like living in an entirely different house—new rooms, a new office.

He just wondered if he was going to see Casey in every room? This was *his* house, and yet there was a strange sort of intimacy in knowing that she'd had a part in its plan and design. Would he ever be able to forget that it was her hand that had brought blueprints and a pile of lumber to life, her hand that had built and molded his house into a home?

He headed down the drive toward the shed. Of course he knew the construction on the house was going to attract a lot of attention today. Almost everyone he knew was aware of the expansion and often would ask questions about the plans and the progress. Maybe it was just as well that Casey would be there. At least she could answer the questions—even walk those interested through the frame for a tour.

Still, it was a hell of a price to pay. If there was one thing he'd learned in the last four weeks, it was that avoiding her was the safest thing to do. Something happened to him when she was around. He acted as if he'd never been around a woman before. The more he was around her, the more he learned about her, and the harder it was for him to keep a perspective on things. It was as if he was a kid again—with hormones surging unchecked through his system and his glands ruling his life.

He pulled open the shed door, pushing the wheelbarrow inside and resting it against the wall. He glanced down at the large tin of charcoal starter, but made no move to bend down and pick it up. He forgot for a moment about grilling time and the shower that he needed. He was thinking about her lips and how smooth and full they had looked that morning in front of his house.

He'd wanted to kiss her that morning. In fact, he couldn't remember having wanted to kiss a woman more. He could still remember the softness of her hand in his, the delicate fragrance of her hair and the moist fullness of her mouth. He'd wanted to kiss her all right, and he would have, too, if Jenny hadn't come tearing out of the front door and interrupted them.

Colt thought of his little girl, and a mixture of relief and regret stirred in his heart. Jenny couldn't have picked a better time to interrupt them if she'd tried. Coming out of the house at that particular moment had broken the spell the way nothing else could have. And like it or not, he'd spent the last week moving back and forth between being annoyed with her and being grateful. Jenny just might have saved him from making one of the biggest mistakes of his life.

He couldn't help wondering just what would have happened had he kissed her that morning, if he'd grabbed her up into his arms and pressed his mouth to hers as he'd so desperately wanted to do? Where would it have led—to a bed, to an affair?

He shook his head. He wasn't prepared to get involved. He didn't want a woman in his life—and certainly not on any kind of permanent basis. And Casey Sullivan was hardly the kind of woman a man would look to for a one-night stand.

Colt reached down and snatched up the tin of charcoal starter and pushed his way out of the shed. He shouldn't have insisted that she join them for the barbecue. He should have given himself a little breathing space away from her, not look for more ways to spend time with her.

"Daddy, come on," Jenny called from the back porch. "Emma said you better get in here and take a shower. Everybody's going to be here soon."

Colt gave her a wave and nodded his head. "Tell Emma I'm almost done. I'll be up in just a minute."

He doused the charcoal, bringing it to flame with a drop of a match. After waiting until the flames had burned down and the edges of the coals had begun to turn white, he headed back toward the house.

Actually the last thing he was in the mood for at the moment was a houseful of people. He felt more like finding a dark corner somewhere and hiding out for a while, trying to purge himself of her image, until he could start thinking straight again. He'd screwed up once, had allowed himself to get roped into a relationship and into a marriage before he'd known what was happening, and he couldn't afford to let that happen again.

"What are you doing here?"

Casey looked up from her desk and gave her brother a careless glance. "I could ask you the same thing."

Bobby Sullivan lifted his chin, motioning to the file cabinet along the wall. "My boss told me I had to have those plans for the minimart finished by the end of next week or she'd chew me out good."

Casey made a face, knowing that wasn't the reason, but also knowing better than to push. It was four years ago, on the way home from a Fourth of July fireworks display at the county fairgrounds, that a drunk driver had plowed into Bobby's car, killing his wife Connie and their little boy Sam. The holiday had become a rough one for him, but since he'd stopped drinking, it had been important that he get through it alone.

"Chew you out," she said, laughing. "That will be the day."

Bobby laughed, walking around the desk beside hers and lowering himself into the chair. The offices of Sullivan Construction were small and cramped, and his big frame seemed to swallow up what vacant space there was.

"Oh, don't let her looks fool you," he said, leaning back and propping his heels up on the desk. "Old Lady Sullivan can be a real tiger when she wants to be."

"Old Lady Sullivan," she mumbled, knowing how Bobby loved to tease her. She flipped her heavy ponytail back and made a waving gesture at his feet on the desk. "And if Myra sees you with your feet on her desk, she'll be the one doing the chewing."

Bobby's face quickly sobered. Myra Crumb had been the secretary and receptionist for Sullivan Construction for as far back as either of them could remember, and crossing her was never a pleasant experience. Bobby lifted his boots off the desk and slipped them back onto the floor.

"I thought you were going to something up at the Wyatt place today—a big to-do or something."

Casey leaned back in her chair. "Oh, I am, I am. But it's not for a little while yet."

"Then what are you doing here?"

She flipped the pages of the folder spread out on the desk in front of her. "We got those new payroll deduction forms from the insurance company I've been wanting to take a look at, and Myra has been after me to read through the new state-comp reports we got back from Sacramento."

"And you're doing that today? What for?"

Casey gave her brother a cool look, remembering that when he'd been drinking these were just the kinds of details he'd frequently let slide. "It needs doing, that's why."

But if she'd meant to intimidate him, it didn't work. He leaned back in the chair and raised his arms up, cradling his head in his hands. "That's busy work, little sister," he pointed out, arching a skeptical brow. "Sounds to me like you're trying awfully hard to look for something to do."

Casey glanced down at the pile of papers before her and gave her shoulder a careless shrug. He was right, of course. She had been looking for something—anything actually—that would keep her mind occupied and stop her from thinking about the barbecue this afternoon.

She thought back to that early morning a week ago, and Jenny's sudden and exuberant invitation. It all seemed pretty much a blur to her now. First there had been Colt with no shirt on, and then there had been that look in his eyes. Then suddenly he was holding her hand and pulling her to him—saying her name softly over and over again.

Casey gave her head a quick shake. Maybe if she hadn't been so distracted, she would have been able to turn down Jenny's invitation without hurting her feelings. After all, it wouldn't have taken much. She could have just lied, could have just said she was busy or planned to be out of town.

Casey closed her eyes. Of course she could think of a dozen excuses now. But not a week ago. That morning all she'd been able to do was look up into Colt Wyatt's eyes and say yes.

She opened her eyes and rubbed at her throbbing temples. Why had she agreed to go? She didn't want to. She wanted to finish the job on the Wyatt house and move on to something else—something that wasn't going to cause such emotional upheaval. She'd already begun to worry about how much she was going to miss Jenny. Her attachment to the little girl was as unreasonable and out of place in her life as her attraction to Colt, and yet it seemed she had little control over either. In another six weeks her work for the Wyatts would be over. She should be putting distance between herself and the situation—not accepting invitations that would only entangle her more.

"So, you going to tell me, or do I have to guess?"

Casey let her gaze slide to Bobby. "Tell you what?"

"What's got you in here on a holiday looking over payroll deductions."

Casey flipped the folder closed in front of her and heaved a tired sigh. "Just restless. I had some time to kill—thought I'd get some work done, that's all. You know how hard it is to get to the office when you've got a job going."

Bobby's dark eyes narrowed. "So this doesn't have anything to do with Colt Wyatt then, I take it?"

Casey's head reared up. "Of course not. Why would you think something like that?"

Bobby shrugged casually. "No reason. Just that Jake and Ronnie were in yesterday to pick up their paychecks. They seemed to think the two of you might be spending some time together."

Casey felt her cheeks scald bright with color, wondering just how much her crew had seen that morning a week ago. "I didn't realize Jake and Ronnie had so much time on their hands. Maybe I should think about picking up the pace a little—since they seem to like to stand around and gossip like a couple of old women."

"So this barbecue today is just business?"

"Of course it's just business," she insisted, a little too vehemently than she'd meant to. "I mean, the man is our client. And despite what my crew seem to think, it is customary that we talk to our clients from time to time.''

"And the little girl?"

She leaned back in the chair again and folded her arms over her chest. "That must have been some chat the three of you had. Did Jake and Ronnie tell you I sometimes bring junk food in my lunches, too? You going to lecture me about my diet next?"

But Bobby was unfazed by her sarcasm. "It sounded like Wyatt's little girl might be about the age of—"

"Okay, I know where you're going with this," she said, springing forward in her chair and cutting him off. "And you can just stop it right there. I'm not looking for some sort of substitute for the husband and child I lost, if that's what you're getting at.''

"Okay, okay," Bobby said quickly, coming forward in his chair. "Look, I'm sorry. I didn't mean to upset you—"

"I'm not upset," Casey insisted, cutting him off again, but her eyes stung bright with tears. "I'm angry."

"Okay then," Bobby conceded good-naturedly. "I didn't mean to make you angry, either." He rose up off the chair and crossed the small office to where she sat. "I was just concerned, that's all. You're my baby sister—I worry about you. That's what big brothers are supposed to do." He leaned down and gave her a peck on the forehead. "I don't know much about this Wyatt character. I mean he seemed like a stand-up enough sort of guy the few times I met him, but I know how you feel about kids. I didn't want to see you taken advantage of."

Despite her anger, Casey had to laugh at the thought. "Colt Wyatt isn't taking advantage of me," she said, pushing Bobby away and rising to her feet. "And the last thing he wants is a new mother for his little girl. The man's like a bear guarding his den when it comes to Jenny."

"So there's nothing personal between you."

Casey picked up her purse and headed for the door. "No, nothing personal."

"Well, that's a relief."

She stopped at the door and turned around, giving him a quizzical look. "What's that supposed to mean?"

Bobby straightened up and walked to the file cabinet, resting a casual arm atop it. "Well, just that if it was personal, I sure as hell wouldn't wear *that*."

Casey looked down at the khaki shorts and pale yellow polo shirt she had on. "What's the matter with what I've got on?"

"Nothing," Bobby said, making a shooing motion with his hand. "It's great, as long as it's business I'd say shorts and a ponytail were just fine."

"And if it wasn't?"

Bobby straightened up, the beginning of a smile cracking across his lips. "You said there was nothing—"

"There *is* nothing," Casey said with an impatient wave of her hand. "But I'm curious. What difference would it make if there were?"

Bobby shrugged innocently, but his smile broke into a full grin. "Well, none really, but I know if I was interested in a woman who dressed like a man every day, I'd sure as hell appreciate seeing her look like a girl once in a while."

"Don't look now, but I think one's about to get away from you there."

Colt turned at the sound of Elias's voice behind him. "Hmm...what?"

Elias pointed to the grill, where one rack of ribs had begun to fall through the grate and was perched precariously over the glowing coals.

"Damn," Colt muttered, taking the long tongs and lifting the meat back into place.

"A little distracted are we?" Elias asked, nodding his head in the direction of the striped canopy on the lawn.

Colt frowned, following Elias's line of vision to the large group gathered beneath the striped canopy. But he knew it wasn't the group his friendly veterinarian was referring to, but rather one member in particular.

Casey Sullivan stood in the middle of the crowd, talking and laughing and looking a little like the belle of the ball. Only she didn't look much like "Casey" this afternoon. There was no hard hat, no chambray shirt or jeans, no heavy work boots. In a soft sea green sundress that left her arms and shoulders bare, and with her hair falling loose and free down her back, she looked delicate and feminine. Casey the construction worker had taken the day off, and Cassandra had taken her place.

"I was, uh, just looking for Jenny," he lied, feeling the muscles around his stomach tighten into a knot.

"Yeah, you and every man in a ten-mile radius," Elias snorted dryly, giving his eyes a slight roll. "I told you she was something, didn't I?"

Colt glared at Elias, suddenly and uncomfortably aware of the heat from the coals against his face. "Cool down, Doc, and you better stop drooling or you'll put out the charcoal."

Elias laughed and gave Colt a sidelong glance. "What's the matter, cowboy, did you stake a claim? Am I getting a little too close to your filly?"

"She's hardly my *filly*," Colt snapped, setting the tongs aside and stepping back from the fire. "I've staked no claim. You want the lady, go for it."

"Oh, right," he snorted. "As if a pretty young thing like her would look twice at an old coot like me." He sighed wistfully as he gazed back across the lawn. "Mind you, if I was twenty years younger, I'd take you up on that offer. I'd be all over her like ants at a picnic."

Colt picked up the tongs and turned to the meat on the grill again, grateful when Elias's attention was diverted elsewhere by some of the other guests. He wasn't interested in continuing their conversation. In fact, at the moment he wasn't entirely sure he was interested in talking to Elias Milton ever again—at least not about Casey Sullivan, anyway.

Colt thought of his blithe responses to Elias about having no interest in the woman. Who did he think he was kidding? If only that were true. If only he could be so casual as to hand her off to someone else. But the fact of the matter was that the thought of her in the arms of another man had his body growing hot again—heat that had nothing to do with the blazing sun or the burning coals.

He turned and glanced across the yard to where she stood chatting with his Aunt Mary. Watching the two, he would have thought they were old friends by the way they visited so easily together. She seemed to have worked her magic on everyone. Jenny had hardly left her side all day, and even old Mac, who normally had little time for the social graces or the fairer sex, hovered close by looking courtly and downright attentive.

Turning back to the grill, Colt reached for the long-handled brush, which was drenched with spicy barbecue sauce, and slathered the ribs once again. She'd made quite an impression on everyone all right—and he hadn't been immune himself.

He remembered when she'd arrived, when he'd looked up and spotted her truck pulling onto the drive. She'd managed to render him almost catatonic when she'd stepped out and headed down the walk toward him. In a hard hat and jeans she'd managed to stir him up pretty well. But in a sundress that hugged her breasts tightly and flowed down her hips in a soft cloud of color and motion, she'd practically brought him to his knees. It was all he could do to remember his own name let alone hers, when it came time for introductions to be made.

He'd taken refuge at the barbecue pit after that and stayed there. It kept his mind occupied and gave him an excuse to keep his distance.

"Need some help?"

He turned around, looking down into her soft eyes. He gripped the handle of the brush even tighter. "No thanks," he said, giving his head a shake. It was hot in front of the fire, but it was a different kind of heat that crawled up his belly now. He dipped the brush back into the bucket of sauce and dabbed the meat again. "I think it's pretty much under control."

Casey leaned forward a little, peering down at the mountain of ribs that lined the huge grill. "Smells wonderful. Everyone's been saying your barbecues are famous."

Colt shrugged, wondering what else she'd been hearing about him. "You know what they say," he said, holding up the brush. "The secret's in the sauce."

She nodded, watching as he drenched the ribs in the rich, red sauce again. "I didn't get a chance before," she started to say after a moment. "To thank you...for the invitation, I mean. It was nice of you to include me."

Colt dropped the brush back into the bucket and reached for a towel. "I'm...I'm glad you could make it," he said awkwardly, wondering what it was about her that had him acting like a tongue-tied idiot. "I'm sorry your brother couldn't make it."

"Yes, I know," she said. "But the Fourth of July isn't one of his favorite holidays."

"Doesn't like the Fourth?" He laughed, wiping his hands on the towel and tossing it aside. "What? Did he have a bad experience with a firecracker when he was a kid?"

"No," she said, grimacing just a little. "With a drunk driver."

Colt felt all the air leave his lungs in one long, painful breath. He'd barely been with the woman for two minutes and he'd already made a fool of himself.

"Oh God, Casey, I'm sorry. Elias told me about the accident and Bob's loss. I'm really sorry—"

"No," she said, shaking her head. Why had she even mentioned the accident? It was obvious he felt terrible, and all she'd succeeded in doing was to embarrass him. "It's fine, really."

"But it was a stupid thing to say," he insisted. "I'm really sorry."

"No, Colt. Really," she persisted, her hand reaching up and making contact with his chest. "Don't apologize. You didn't know."

Somehow his hand had found hers, as it rested along the front of his shirt, and covered it completely. He suddenly forgot about not wanting her in his life, forgot about all the good, solid reasons he had for steering clear. It was as if the noisy crowd of friends filling his backyard had disappeared and he was left alone with her.

"Why is it I always seem to say the wrong thing when you're around?"

"Is that what you do?" Casey felt her heart stumble in her chest, and emotion made the words come out in a whispery rush.

of tension around his chest grew tighter. For some unfathomable reason, it hadn't seemed to bother him that people had been watching, that his friends and family had seen them together and tongues had been wagging ever since. What was the matter with him? Why wasn't he avoiding her like the plague instead of looking for excuses to be with her?

He watched as she stepped back from the pit, exchanging a "high five" with Mary and Jenny and several ardent female supporters from the crowd that had gathered. Even now, she had a smooth, graceful sort of elegance about her. He realized it would almost be worth losing a round of play just to see the way her body moved when she tossed the shoes.

"I believe it's your turn," Mary Wyatt called to him with mock innocence. She smiled sweetly at her husband and nephew, but her eyes shone with humor. "Unless, of course, you'd like to throw in the towel now."

There was a loud rumble of laughter from the cluster of friends who had gathered to watch. The crowd had split pretty much along gender lines, and there were a lot of good-natured barbs passed back and forth between the two groups. Caught up in the lighthearted teasing, Colt raised his set of horseshoes in a challenging salute.

"You don't close the corral gate until the last mare is in," he said, finding Casey's soft, brown eyes in the crowd.

Casey met his cool, blue gaze, feeling the pulse at her neck beat hard and fast. She suddenly remembered something Bobby had said years before. He and his friends had been joking, talking about girls getting involved in sports, and they'd all agreed no boy would want a girl who could beat him at his favorite sport.

The statement had infuriated her at the time—it still did, for that matter. The idea that girls were expected to downplay their natural abilities in order to build a man's ego had been something she'd never accepted. She'd never given in, had always fought hard and played to win.

Still, as she watched Colt step up to the mark and take careful aim at the spike, she had to wonder. Maybe it wouldn't have hurt just this once to have toned it down a little.

But then she gave her head a shake, dispelling the silly thought. Colt Wyatt was hardly the kind of man whose ego had to be built up and bolstered by anyone. She couldn't imagine him being intimidated by anyone—least of all over a game of horseshoes. That simply wasn't his style. He was too strong, too confident to need anything like that.

Colt let the first horseshoe fly, sending it high into the air. With absolute accuracy, it settled around the spike onto the sand with a solid thud. It was only then that Casey realized she had been holding her breath, and she released it in a long, slow sigh. She watched as he began lining up his second shot, pausing for a moment to give her a brief look.

Casey's breath caught in her throat, and embarrassingly she felt her face flush with heat. What was happening to her? She was practically swooning, and it had to stop. People were beginning to notice. Already Mary Wyatt had been making some not-so-subtle observations and drawing conclusions that were completely incorrect—like mentioning how long it had been since Colt's wife died, how much Jenny needed a mother, and how the spare room next to Jenny's in the new wing would make a perfect nursery.

But even as she reminded herself how important it was to keep some perspective, she found herself thinking about the look she had seen in his eyes. "Pretty"...he had said she looked pretty, and for some ridiculous reason that made her feel like smiling. It had been such a nice thing to say, a sweet compliment—like a kiss on the hand. She'd had men tell her she was beautiful, that she was sexy and a babe—but pretty?

She smiled. When Colt Wyatt had looked into her eyes, had pressed a sweet, innocent kiss along her hand, she'd actually *felt* pretty.

Colt's second shot with the horseshoe was another ringer, and the crowd hooted and cheered. Casey felt her pulse pound in her ears, giving him a silent applause with her hands when he turned his blue gaze to her. This next shot would decide it.

He glanced up, looking at her from the far side of the horseshoe pit. A slow smile began to break across his lips as he straightened his tall frame. Turning in her direction, he lifted his arm and casually tossed the shoe in the vague direction of the spike. Everyone—including Casey—gasped with surprise, shocked to see what looked like a purposeful move on his part to throw the game their way.

But there must have been a method to his madness. With the horseshoe still wobbling through the air, Colt started across the pit, his long strides bringing him to within inches of her. He hesitated for a moment, staring down at her, waiting for the sound he seemed certain would come.

And then it did. The horseshoe found its target with unerring accuracy. The clank of steel to steel brought the house down.

"Winner, and still champion," he murmured, just loud enough for her to hear. "Kiss me, Casey. I've come to claim my prize."

Caught up in the moment, Casey didn't even think twice. In the middle of the chaos around them, with all the laughing and the cheering and applause from those all about, she rose up on tiptoe and planted a firm kiss squarely on his cheek.

"Yup," old Mac said, walking up from behind and putting a hand on each of their shoulders. "The way you two throw shoes, you're a natural team—there'd be no stoppin' you."

Casey slipped the long leather strap of her purse over her shoulder. It was late. The afternoon had been a long and busy one. But oddly enough, she felt anything but exhausted. She felt invigorated. After the horseshoe competition, there had been s'mores in front of the camp fire, and sparklers to light up the night. Only it was after ten now, and as much as she would have liked this day to have gone on forever, the festivities had begun to wind down. The charcoal had long turned to ashes, the tiki torches were burning low, and the hot summer night was turning balmy. Many of the guests had begun to gather up their things and head for the long line of cars that bordered the front drive, carrying their sleepy children in their arms.

Casey scanned the yard, looking for Colt and Jenny. They'd been there just a short time ago—Colt carrying a tired Jenny on his shoulders. But Harry and Pat McKenna from the horsemen's association had walked up and begun asking her questions about adding a room addition onto their home, and she'd become distracted. When she'd finally looked again, neither Colt nor Jenny were anywhere in sight. She wanted to say good-night, to thank them both for the invitation, for the wonderful day, but she couldn't find them anywhere.

"It's been quite a day."

Casey turned to Mary Wyatt, who walked slowly across the yard. "Quite a day," she said, nodding her head in agreement. "Have you seen Jenny or Colt around?"

Mary glanced about, her eyes squinting in the darkness. "Come to think of it, I haven't." Her frown deepened. "Now where do you suppose those two have gotten to?"

"Well, it's not important," Casey said, making a dismissive gesture with her hand. "I just wanted to say good-night."

"You're not leaving yet, are you?"

Casey smiled. "It's late, and don't forget I'm a working girl."

Mary turned and looked up at the dark skeleton of the house's half-finished wing. "I still find it hard to believe you can do something like that—hammers, saws, drills," she said with a shake of her head. "But then, I guess a woman who can toss a horseshoe and make those two egomaniacs of mine sweat, the way you did, can do just about anything she pleases."

Casey laughed, remembering how pleased Mary had been with the results of their game of horseshoes. They might have lost their challenge to Colt and his Uncle Sid, but they'd given them a run for their money. "Well, not *anything*."

Mary turned and looked back up at the half-built wing. "How much longer—until it's finished, I mean?"

Casey followed Mary's line of vision and looked up at the dark structure. Only she wasn't thinking about the insulation that hadn't arrived yet, or the electrical subcontractor who was giving her trouble about the light fixtures Colt had chosen for the bathroom. She was thinking about getting back to business, about finishing up one job and getting started on another. After tonight, there would be no sundresses and kisses on the hand—just a work shirt, a hard hat and a tool belt.

She glanced down at her hands, clenched tightly together in front of her. It was a little hard for a man to kiss a woman's hand when it was covered with a work glove.

"I promised Colt we'd have it done by the time Jenny's ready for school at the end of next month," she finally said after a moment. "About six weeks, I guess."

"Six weeks," Mary murmured, slowly turning to Casey. "And then what? Another job?"

Casey nodded thoughtfully. How many times had she started a new job, seen it through to completion and then moved on to the next? Already she'd made an appointment with the McKennas for Bobby to go out and give them a bid on a room addition. One job after the other—that was the transient nature of the business—the business she'd known all her life.

So why, then, did it make her want to cry when she heard Mary Wyatt say it? Was it because this time she would be leaving behind more than a finished job— because she'd be leaving Jenny and Colt?

"Yes," she said quietly. All of the excitement of the day had suddenly disappeared, leaving her feeling drained and alone. "Another job."

"Well I can tell you one thing—it's been quite an experience for Jenny. It's all she's talked about for weeks. And the tour she gave Sid and me earlier—" Mary threw her head back and laughed. "You should have seen Sid's expression when she stood there in that hard hat and tool belt and explained to him about laying down a subfloor." Her shoulders shook from the laughter, and her eyes filled with tears. "I swear, it was just about the sweetest thing I ever saw."

Casey smiled as she listened to Mary, but the lump of emotion in her throat was almost too much to handle.

"She's made the job pretty special for all of us," Casey admitted, taking a deep breath. Suddenly it had become very important that she get out of there, before she got really depressed and did something stupid—like cry. "Well, I really have to be going. Mary, would you mind thanking Jenny for me? And Colt, too, of course. Please tell them I had a wonderful time."

"I wouldn't mind a bit." Mary smiled, giving her a hug. "And I'll tell you a little secret," she said in a stage whisper. "I think having you here made it more fun for everyone—especially Colt."

Casey felt her cheeks flush and her stomach roll uneasily. She knew she should correct Mary, should make some attempt to set the record straight. Because despite the magic of the afternoon, despite how much she dreamed or how much she would have wanted it to be, the fact remained that Colt Wyatt was her employer—nothing more. Colt had been the charming host, going out of his way to make her feel relaxed and welcome. And she'd found herself captivated by it all, caught up in the attention and fireworks of the moment, and forgetting all about what was real. But just like Cinderella, her fantasy had come to an end. The clock had struck twelve and the world was turning back into a pumpkin.

"Good night, Mary," Casey whispered quickly in a thick, raspy voice. "And please, give Jenny a hug for me."

She took off across the yard and headed toward the drive. She must be tired, must be suffering the side effects of too much sun, too many people and too much to eat. What else could it be? What else could explain why she was such an emotional wreck? It had been one afternoon—a pleasant social engagement with a client. So why did she suddenly feel as though

she were the heroine in some kind of tragic melo-
drama, who was being torn from those she loved?

Casey stopped short. From those she loved? She
had to end this, had to start putting things in perspective. Loving Jenny was one thing. She was a sweet little girl. Everyone who knew her loved her. But
Colt...that was something else entirely. How could she
be in love with him? Was the feeling in her heart real,
or was she simply daydreaming again?

"Hey, lady, want a lift?"

Casey whirled around, startled by Colt's voice and
the mélange of noises coming from behind her.

"Come on, Casey," Jenny shouted, leaning down
out of the old-fashioned horse-drawn buggy and
looking far too alert and wide awake for a five-year-
old at ten o'clock in the evening. "Go for a ride with
Daddy and me."

"A ride," Casey repeated skeptically as Colt
brought the buggy to a stop beside her. "In that
thing?"

"Sure." Jenny giggled, scooting over on the small
bench to make room. "It's fun."

"Well, thanks for the offer," Casey said, shifting
her gaze to Colt. "But I think I'll pass on this one."
She turned back to Jenny, reaching up and giving her
upturned nose an affectionate tap. "And shouldn't
you be in bed, young lady? I think those lids of yours
are looking awfully droopy."

"I'm not sleepy," Jenny insisted, shaking her head.
She turned and gave her father a quick look. "Honest, I'm not sleepy." She turned back to Casey.

"Please come, okay? Daddy says we'll show you the pond."

"Thanks, sweetie," Casey said, patting Jenny's arm. "But it's pretty late, and I really should be going." She leaned close and gave Jenny a conspiratorial wink. "Besides, I have to get to the job site early in the morning or the man I'm working for just might fire me."

"Oh, Casey." Jenny giggled. "Daddy won't fire you."

"I don't know," Casey said skeptically, glancing up at Colt again. "I hear he's a pretty tough customer."

"Only when it comes to horseshoes," Colt pointed out, the slightest hint of a smile showing at the corners of his mouth. "Otherwise, he's a pussycat."

"A pussycat, huh?" Casey mused. "Why do I find that hard to believe?"

Colt shrugged. "Beats me. As a matter of fact, I hear he's a prince of a guy. Now hop aboard."

Casey laughed, but shook her head. "Thanks, but I'd better not."

"Come on, Casey, it's a special night," Colt said, reaching around his daughter and extending his hand out to her. "Please."

Casey looked up into Colt's eyes and felt all the breath seep out of her lungs. It would be a mistake to go. Any further involvement would only make breaking away that much harder to do. She knew all the risks, recognized the dangers and understood the need for caution.

Which is why she would never understand how her hand found its way into his.

She felt the warm roughness of his palm, felt the strength in his arm and his hand when he pulled her up and into the seat beside him.

She was going to get hurt, Casey thought, as Jenny settled herself onto her lap and cuddled close. She knew it and yet she was completely unwilling to do anything to stop it. For better or for worse, she wanted this moment, this night. If there would be hell to pay, she'd pay it later. Right now her world had become the man beside her and his child nestled in her arms.

"Nice," Jenny said with a yawn, looking through the scrub oak to the full moon shining above.

"I thought you said you weren't sleepy," Colt said, looking down into his daughter's relaxed face.

"Not sleepy," Jenny mumbled, reaching up and taking a long lock of Casey's hair and weaving it lazily through her little fingers. "Happy."

Chapter Seven

Happy. Colt considered the warm, pleasant sensation swelling in his chest. Was that what he was feeling right now? Had it been so long, he didn't recognize the feeling anymore?

He tugged slightly on the left side of Snapper's reins, and the shiny chestnut stallion responded immediately to the directive, guiding the buggy carefully around the crumbling edges of the ditch. Both man and horse knew the well-worn trail that wound through the woods behind the stables and led to the pond in the meadow beyond. They had made the trip down the narrow, rutted path together many times in the past, and long ago committed to memory every bump, every pothole, and every loose patch of gravel.

Colt reached up and braced himself for the bend in the road, a turn to the right that would bring them out of the woods and into the clearing. But even though Snapper had slowed his pace automatically in anticipation of the move, the curve brought Casey sliding close on the small bench, causing the weight of her body to press close to his.

Happy, he thought as he felt Casey's warmth against him. He turned his head, catching a glimpse of her in the corner of his eye. When was the last time he'd asked a woman to join him on a buggy ride in the moonlight?

Just then Casey shifted, the soft rustle of the cotton sundress along his leg causing the warmth in his body to edge up a degree.

He'd told her tonight had been a special one, but he wondered if she had any idea just how special it really was. He'd stormed barriers today and broken new ground. He didn't bring women to his home, didn't invite them to spend time with his daughter or his friends, didn't challenge them to games of horseshoes and then parade around like a peacock trying to impress them.

And yet today he'd done all those things. Why? Happiness. Somehow, this woman had stepped into his life and made it better. Casey Sullivan made him happy.

"Daddy," Jenny mumbled sleepily. "Are we there yet?"

"Just about, baby," Colt said, looking down at his daughter nestled in Casey's lap.

"Tell Snapper to hurry, Daddy," she said with a yawn. "I want Casey to see the pollywogs."

Colt reached down and ran a gentle finger along her cheek. "Don't worry, Casey will see the pollywogs," he assured her in a soothing voice.

"I brought the flashlight," she said, struggling to sit up.

"I know, I know where it is," he insisted, stopping her with his hand.

Jenny settled back against Casey's arm. "But...but just in case, if I get a little sleepy," she said, and Colt and Casey exchanged a quick, amused look. "If I get sleepy, will you show her?"

"Of course," he said, in a quiet voice. "I'll find some pollywogs for Casey."

Casey looked into Colt's clear blue eyes and felt herself flush warm all over. She glanced down at the child cuddled in her arms. Jenny's struggle to stay awake had been a valiant one, but she'd lost the battle. She'd fallen fast asleep in her arms.

"She gave it her best."

Casey's gaze flickered to Colt, then to the sleeping child in her lap. "Yes, she did. But she had quite a day."

"How about you?"

"I've had quite a day, too."

He glanced back to the trail in front of them and tried not to think about the way the moonlight made her skin look as smooth and as soft as silk. "How was the hayride?"

"Do you realize that was my first?"

"You're kidding," he said, turning to her in disbelief. "You've never been on a hayride before?"

She shook her head. "Never."

He gave her a skeptical look. "How could you have grown up in these foothills and not gone on a hayride?"

Casey laughed. "You forget, I was raised on a construction site, not a horse ranch."

"Well, maybe that could explain it," he admitted, his tone doubtful. "But it still seems a little weird. I mean, what did you and your brother do for fun when you were little, take rides on bulldozers?"

"Hey, bulldozers can be a lot of fun," she insisted, feigning indignation.

"Bulldozers are nothing compared to hayrides."

"Oh, yeah?"

"Yeah."

She thought a minute and then shrugged. "Yeah, you're right. Hayrides have it all over bulldozers—but circular saws—circular saws are really fun."

He laughed, regarding her for a moment and enjoying the joking. "So how'd you like your first hayride?"

"Actually, I loved it," Casey said, meaning it. She thought about the huge tractor-driven flatbed trailer and children and the crazy songs they all had sung. She gave her head a shake. "Except I think I'll be picking straw out of my hair for the next week."

As if to help demonstrate her point, Colt leaned close, reaching out and plucking a small piece from a strand of her long hair. "I don't think hay scratches so much when you're a kid."

Casey gave her head a small shake, suspiciously eyeing the ends of her hair. "That's nice to know."

He reached down and pulled a sizable piece of straw from the cuff of Jenny's shorts. "See what I mean?"

They both laughed then, causing Jenny to stir. But after another big yawn, the sleepy little girl snuggled close and fell back to sleep again. Gradually their laughter died, and they rode along in silence—with only the sounds of the meadow and Snapper's steady hoofbeats breaking through the moonlit night.

"I had a really nice afternoon," Casey said after a while, keeping her eyes on the sleeping child in her arms. "Thank you."

"You're making it sound like the evening has come to an end," Colt said, bringing Snapper to a stop at the edge of the pond.

"Well, it is late," she said.

Colt smiled, reached down and set the brake of the buggy. "I promised Jenny you'd see pollywogs," he said, jumping down from the buggy.

Casey laughed as he grabbed a blanket from the back. Spreading it out behind the seat, he lifted Jenny out of her arms and settled the sleeping child on top of it, making a snug bed.

Pulling a flashlight out from beneath the small bench, he lifted a gentlemanly hand to Casey. "Madam, your frog babies await."

Casey gingerly leaned forward, peering down into the small pool of water that had been trapped between the rocks. In it a multitude of tiny creatures swam through the circle of light made by the flashlight's beam. Pollywogs. Like hayrides, they were another common childhood experience that seemed to have eluded her.

She watched the pollywogs dart in and out of view, the light glowing against their slick, wet bodies and reflecting back in a myriad of tiny specks of color.

"You know, they're actually cute."

Colt looked up. "You sound surprised."

"I am, I guess," she admitted. "I mean they grow up to be big, yucky, ugly frogs."

Colt watched the way the breeze moved through the long tresses of her hair. "Frogs aren't ugly."

"Oh, yes they are," Casey stated flatly, nodding her head.

He gave her a dubious look. "Have you ever actually seen a frog? I mean up front and personal?"

"Yes I've *seen* a frog," she insisted, mimicking his tone. "And more personally than I care to remember."

"Oh?"

She saw his curious expression and smiled. "My brother and his friends used to catch them all the time. They kept them as pets and jumped them at the annual Calavaras frog jumping contest at Angels Camp every year. They were always threatening to put them in my bath water, or in my bed." She gave her head another shake and shivered. "Of course, I would never let them know it bothered me. That would have only made things worse, but I can't tell you how many nights I woke up scared to death that I would find one of those bulgy-eyed creatures staring at me. So, yes, I know all about frogs, and they're slimy, their skin feels gross—and they're ugly."

Colt smiled, imagining what a scrappy little girl she must have been. He leaned down and scooped up a handful of water, gathering several pollywogs in his palms. "Want to touch one?"

"No," Casey said, rearing back. "No, thank you."

He looked up. "Why not? I thought you said they were cute."

"They are cute, but I'm not touching one."

"Jenny does all the time."

She gave him a deliberate look. "And that's supposed to intimidate me?"

"No," he laughed, giving his head a shake. He let the water pour from his hands, returning the pollywogs to the pool. "I'm just surprised, that's all."

"Oh?" she asked, feeling herself flush despite the cool night air. "What about?"

He wiped his hands together. "Well, you work a tough job in construction, handle a power saw better than any man I've ever seen, and drive a half-ton pickup truck down these country roads like it was a sports car, but the thought of touching a little pollywog grosses you out."

Casey straightened up, bristling, and came slowly to her feet. "So according to you, since I do a man's job, frogs and pollywogs shouldn't bother me?"

Colt stood up, stepping over the pool to where she stood. "You're not going to get prickly on me again, are you?"

"Prickly?"

"Yes, prickly," he repeated, reaching for her hand. "I thought we got all that sexist stuff straightened out a long time ago."

"Did we?" Casey asked in a tight voice. She tried to pull her hand free of his hold, but he wouldn't let go.

"Yes," he murmured, pulling her close. "We did."

"Then what does my working in construction have anything to do with me not liking frogs?" She still struggled, shifting back a step. She'd chosen to take offense, to bristle at his remarks. After all, if she were angry, she wouldn't have to think about where she was, and how he was looking at her.

"Nothing," he whispered, slipping a hand on her waist and edging her closer to him. "Except I can't imagine anything big brother Bobby would do that his scrappy little sister wouldn't want in on, too."

"Oh," Casey murmured, looking up into his eyes and trying to remember what it was she was so upset about in the first place. He wasn't insulting her, wasn't making a crack about her job, and she knew it. He was just teasing her.

"Casey," he whispered, slipping his arms around her waist and pulling her close. "Beautiful Casey. What are we doing? Why are we fighting so hard?"

"Colt, please," she struggled, ignoring his question and pushing her palms flat against the hard surface of his chest. "Don't do this."

"Don't do what—touch you, hold you?" He pressed a kiss into the slope of her neck... and then another, and another, and another after that. "How do I stop, Casey? You drive me crazy. I can't think anymore, I can't eat, can't sleep. All I can think about is you."

"No," she moaned, her struggles only settling her more securely into his embrace. "Colt, no, this can't be happening."

"But it is happening," he murmured, moving slowly and deliberately against her. "Casey, I want you. I've wanted you from the first moment I saw you." He brushed his lips softly against hers. "Tell me that it's okay, Casey. Tell me you want me, too."

"No, Colt," she moaned, feeling the heat from his body flowing into hers. "I—I can't—"

"Tell me, Casey," he whispered, his hand moving over the thin fabric of her dress, pressing her close. "Let me hear you say the words."

Casey felt dizzy and light-headed, like she was being catapulted forward at a speed faster than sound, faster than light. She needed time to think, to weigh all the issues and consider all the ramifications—but she'd had weeks to contemplate and convince herself and it had done no good. She was on a collision course, racing through the night toward something she had told herself she had to avoid, but had been wanting all along.

"Oh, yes," she murmured in a voice that sounded foreign to her own ears. "Yes, Colt, I want you."

His mouth found hers, sinking hard and deep, thrusting her lips apart and taking what little sanity she had left. It was all Casey could do to remember to breathe. This was no sweet kiss, no gentle exploration of seek and discover. It was a total capture. She felt breathless and dazed, and it was all she could do to hang on for dear life.

Colt felt the spark in his belly burst into flame. Need exploded into an inferno. His world became this night, this moon and this woman.

He pulled her close, crushing her to him, wanting to feel more of her. Her taste invaded him, moving through his system like heat through a desert. He couldn't get enough—couldn't be close enough, couldn't taste enough. She wasn't the first woman he'd wanted, but he'd never wanted a woman the way he wanted this one now.

"Casey," he growled, tearing his mouth away and burying his face in the juncture of her neck and shoulder. "Casey."

He breathed in the scent of her, planting soft wet kisses on her skin, in her hair and along her jaw. His hands moved over her, restless and hungry, and his blood flowed like hot, molten lava through his veins. His mouth moved down her neck, pushing aside the thin material of her sundress and exposing her flesh to his hungry gaze.

She was beautiful in the moonlight. Her breasts were round, full and perfect, and the longing that flooded his system bordered on desperation. Lifting her to him, he lowered his lips and paid homage to her beauty.

Casey clung to him, helpless against the onslaught of emotions that assailed her. Nothing had prepared her for this—not life, not experience, not even her wildest dreams. The devastating need, the over-whelming desire she felt streaming from every pore rendered her all but helpless. It was like nothing she'd even known. It seemed to rise up from some hidden place inside of her, a treasure trove of sensation where body joined spirit, heart joined mind.

She wasn't an innocent, she'd known the touch of a man. She'd been married, had shared her bed with a husband for four years. But being with Charlie had never been like this.

Already they had gone far beyond a simple kiss in the moonlight. They'd flown past all those preliminary steps, cutting right to the chase. Colt was making love to her.

And she would have gloried in his lovemaking, would have left inhibition and modesty behind and refused him nothing there in the moonlight . . . except for one thing.

Jenny. The strong maternal feelings she felt for Colt's child were able to do what caution and common sense could not—pierce through that dense cloud of emotion and desire that had engulfed her. It didn't matter what she wanted—how much she desired the man in her arms and the night surrounding them. She couldn't lose sight of the fact that Jenny was asleep nearby.

"Colt," she groaned, feeling his mouth at her breast. "Colt, we can't. We shouldn't."

Colt heard her voice but couldn't seem to make himself understand her words. For the moment he was wholly a carnal creature, capable only of feeling and responding.

"L-listen to me, Colt, please," Casey stammered, placing her hands on his shoulders. "Jenny's with us. We can't forget about Jenny."

Colt's entire system froze. The sound of his daughter's name finally penetrated the thick haze of passion and reached that thin thread of sanity he still had.

"Right," he whispered, letting her body slide slowly over his until her feet touched the ground once again. "Jenny."

"She...she could wake up," Casey murmured, straightening her dress and running a shaky hand through her hair. "We can't let her see us...like this."

"Right," he said again, closing his eyes and pulling in a deep breath. His huge body shuddered, and he struggled for control. He glanced up at the buggy and to his sleeping daughter in the back. Jenny. How could he have forgotten? How could all sane, all rational thought have left him so completely?

He looked down at Casey, felt her body tremble next to his. This woman—the woman he wanted for his own. Kissing her, touching her had made him forget everything else.

Pulling her close again, he let his mouth drift to hers once more. "Come with me, Casey," he murmured against her lips. "Come with me back to my house, to my bed." He brushed a kiss against her lips. "We'll put Jenny to sleep, and my room door has a big lock on it. It will be just you and me." He kissed her, an achingly gentle kiss that was fraught with longing and promise. He was in control now, but desire nipped at the edges of his sanity. "Let me love you as you should be loved...long," he whispered, brushing another feather kiss along her lips, "and slow."

Casey breathed out a long sigh, captivated by this gentle seduction as much as she'd been by the onslaught of emotion. "I wish...I wish I could," she groaned, pushing him back. She stepped back a few steps away from the pond and away from him. "But this...this is moving too fast. I—I've got to have some time, I need to think. We both do."

"Think," he mused, catching her as she stepped up the bank, and pulling her slowly back into his arms. "Do you ever wonder if we think too much? I mean, what's wrong with just feeling? Have we forgotten how good it is just to feel?" He kissed her jaw, her neck, her ear. "Doesn't it feel good, Casey, being here, being together?" He pressed soft kisses into her hair and along her forehead. "Wouldn't it feel good to lie together—to hold each other, to touch?" He found her mouth again. "Wouldn't it *feel* good?"

"Oh, yes," she sighed, closing her eyes to the surge of awareness and desire teeming through her system. For a moment she allowed her mind to wander, picturing in her head what it would be like to have Colt make love to her.

Maybe he was right, maybe she did think too much. She could hardly remember a time when she wasn't concerned about something, when there wasn't a crushing responsibility on her shoulders: the business, the job, the deadline, the equipment, the workers, the weather, Bobby's drinking. On and on and on.

She felt Colt's body pressed tightly against hers, felt it grow rigid and hard for her. What would it be like to lose herself in his passion, to succumb to it and forget about everything else?

But even if she could forget all her responsibilities, there was still something to stop her, still someone to consider and think about.

"No, Colt, we can't," she moaned, tearing her mouth away.

"Yes, we can," he whispered insistently, brushing her mouth with a kiss. "Say you'll stay with me, Casey. Tell me you'll stay."

"No," she said firmly, with what small shred of sanity she had left. She pulled free of his hold, taking a few unsteady steps toward the buggy. The night air felt cool and refreshing against her hot skin, and she drew in several deep breaths. She needed a clear head, needed to think straight—for them both—and she couldn't seem to do that with him touching her. "We can't."

Her words were like an icy stake through the heart, and Colt felt the cold spread through his entire body. "Can't, or won't?"

"How can you ask me that?" She heard the anger in his voice, and a tight band of emotion squeezed at her heart. "Did you think I was pretending just now?"

His dark eyes narrowed. "Were you?"

She reached up, running a hand along his cheek. "You know that's not true."

"Yes, I do," he admitted, the anger leaving as quickly as it came. Catching her hand and planting a kiss along the palm. "Then tell me why it's so impossible, help me to understand. I want you, you want me. What's stopping us from having what we want?"

"This isn't just about us."

"What are you talking about?" he argued. "It's all about us—you and me."

"And Jenny," she added quietly.

"This doesn't involve Jenny," he insisted. "She's got nothing to do with this. She wouldn't even have to know."

"Colt, everything you do involves Jenny," Casey said. "And everything you do affects her—which is exactly why we're both going to climb back into that buggy and why you're going to drive me back to my truck and why I'm going to sleep in my own bed tonight. I won't keep secrets—especially from Jenny."

"Casey, wait," Colt said as she began to move away. He reached out, catching her by the arm. He felt like he was coming out of a dream—dazed and off balance. For the second time that night he'd become so blinded by desire, so intent on having this woman that he'd blocked out everything else—including his child.

What kind of man would forget his own child? What kind of father was he? Jenny was a part of him—like his arms or his legs. He'd been stupid to think inviting a woman into their house—even for one night—wouldn't have affected her. Especially if that woman was Casey.

"Casey," he whispered again. "Thank you."

"For what?" Casey asked, looking up at him.

"For being smart." His hand slid down her arm and he caught her hand up in his. "For thinking when I wasn't, and..." They walked back to the small carriage and peered into the back where Jenny lay sleeping. "And for caring about Jenny's feelings even when I didn't remember to."

"Don't thank me, cowboy," she said, as he helped her up into the buggy. "I'm not going to let anybody hurt that little girl—not even her daddy."

Chapter Eight

"They're pollywogs."

"So they are," Casey said dryly, peering up from the plastic bucket resting in the shade of the porch into Jenny's bright blue eyes. She was glad to finally see Jenny talking. The little girl had been strangely quiet and distracted the past several days, and she was starting to get worried. "What are they doing here?"

"Daddy got them for me 'cause I fell asleep on the Fourth."

The Fourth of July. Casey sighed deeply. That was a date that would never be the same again. It had been three days since that glorious night, but when she thought of Colt, of those magical moments they had shared beneath the stars and the moonlight, she felt herself flush all over. She still had a hard time believing it had really happened—it had been too extraordinary, too much like a dream come true.

She touched a hand to her mouth, remembering waking up that next morning and how red and swollen her lips had been. It had been a long time since she'd been kissed by a man—and certainly no man had ever kissed her the way Colt Wyatt had.

Her fingers traced the outline of her lips. It had been three days, but they still felt sensitive, still tingled. Yet even without that gentle reminder, her heart knew the night had been real.

Casey gave her head a shake, trying without much success to squelch the warm, weak feeling that had invaded her system. She had to pull herself together, had to quit acting like a schoolgirl or Jenny was going to notice, if she hadn't already. It almost made her glad Colt was going to be gone from the house all day.

The days since the barbecue had been pretty intense, dealing with all the new emotions between them. They'd agreed to take it slowly, but agreeing and actually doing it were two very different things.

They'd done their best, but it hadn't been easy. There had been those occasional encounters when they'd found themselves alone; the quick kisses, and the long late-night telephone calls. Still, Casey felt she'd had to be on her guard constantly—especially around Jenny. When he'd told her yesterday about going to Sacramento to meet with the state licensing board for the MLHA's show permit, she'd almost felt relieved. At least she'd have a day to relax.

Casey told herself it was only natural that she would want to share her happiness with Jenny, to make her a part of it. But she also understood the importance of holding back. She and Colt were just starting out; it was too soon to know what was going to happen. She felt it was important that she and Colt understand their own feelings better before getting Jenny's involved. Still, Casey felt awkward; she didn't like keeping secrets.

But despite all that, Casey couldn't remember a time when she'd felt happier. Colt had been warm and attentive and wonderful. She remembered how he had walked her to her truck on the night of the Fourth. It had been late, and he'd been concerned about her driving the country roads alone.

Casey felt a warm glow spread through her again as she remembered his concern. He'd wanted to follow her home, wanted to see for himself that she had arrived safely home. It had been such an gallant gesture, so sweet and mannerly she'd almost hated to refuse him.

But she had refused. Being alone with him at her small apartment would have been a disaster. Without Jenny's presence, it would have been too easy for things to have gotten out of control.

Casey closed her eyes, thinking about the long afternoon and the long evening ahead of her. With Colt out of town and gone from the ranch, there would be no chance encounters, no stolen moments or secret telephone calls, and she couldn't help feeling a twinge of regret. As difficult as it was to keep her feelings in check when he was around, being without him wasn't much better.

"He didn't sleep much last night."

Casey jumped, pulled abruptly from her reverie and sending her thoughts scattering in a hundred different directions. "Your daddy?"

"Yeah," Jenny nodded seriously. "I was real sleepy when he came in to say goodbye this morning, but Emma told me at breakfast he was all locked up."

Casey's brow furrowed as she looked into Jenny's big blue eyes. "Locked up?"

"Uh-huh," Jenny said, nodding again. "That's what she said. Daddy was all...locked up." Her voice trailed off and she made a face. "I . . . I think."

"Locked up," Casey repeated, concentrating. Suddenly she looked up, snapping her fingers. "You sure she didn't say he was *keyed* up?"

Jenny's eyes widened, and her mouth broke into a grin. "Yeah, keyed up. That's what she said—Daddy was keyed up." She giggled at her own mistake.

Casey couldn't help smiling herself. She'd spent the last several nights pretty "locked up" herself.

"That's why he got up real early and went down to the pond—'cause he was all keyed up," Jenny went on, dipping her finger into the water and tickling a pollywog. It wiggled wildly, scooting across the bucket with a tiny splash. "We're going to take them over to Mrs. Spagnolia at the Science Center. There's a pond there, too, in the back, and Mrs. Spagnolia collects pollywogs from all over the county to live there." Jenny stopped and looked up at Casey, her eyes squinting against the sun. "Daddy said you wouldn't touch them."

Casey made a face. "I knew I should have sworn him to secrecy."

Jenny laughed as she leaned down and touched the tail of the pollywog again. "They won't hurt you, you know."

"No," Casey mused, making a face. "I don't suppose they would. But you have to admit they look a little slimy."

"No, they don't," Jenny insisted, following them with her finger. "They look soft. See?"

"Yeah," Casey mumbled, unconvinced. She knelt down, peering into the bucket. Why was she being such a chicken? "Maybe."

"They are," Jenny maintained, catching a pollywog between her two fingers and stroking it carefully. "Come on. Look, I've got one. Give him a little pet—see for yourself."

Casey gave Jenny a doubtful look as she gingerly reached her hand into the bucket. "Did your father put you up to this?"

"No." Jenny laughed, taking Casey's finger and gently touching it to the side of the pollywog. "See how soft?"

"Soft," Casey muttered, making a face. She lifted her hand out of the water, standing up and wiping it on the leg of her jeans. "But a little slimy, too."

Jenny laughed again, and let go of the pollywog. "Yeah, maybe a little slimy, too." She stood up and wiped her hands dry on her pant leg just as she'd seen Casey do. "You helped put me to bed the other night, didn't you?"

Casey's hand hesitated as she reached for her tool belt from the back step. Was that why Jenny had been acting differently the past few days? "How did you know that? I thought you were supposed to be asleep."

"Daddy told me."

"Oh?" Casey mumbled thoughtfully as she slipped the belt around her waist. She'd almost managed to convince herself that Jenny's moodiness had merely been a product of her own paranoia, but now she wasn't so sure. "What else did your daddy tell you?"

Jenny reached for her empty thermos and fitted it back into place in her lunch box. "That he thought you looked real pretty in a dress." She snapped the lunch box closed. "And that you and me were just about the prettiest girls he'd ever seen."

Casey's hand slipped on the belt and she dropped one end, sending the hammer and her screwdriver flying to the ground. Maybe this wasn't a conversation she was ready to have just now.

"Darn," she muttered, flustered. She moved to pick them up. "Sounds like you and your daddy had quite a little talk."

"We talk all the time," Jenny said simply, but the little line along her forehead deepened.

"Oh," Casey mumbled, reaching purposefully for the end of the belt. It didn't take a genius to see that Jenny had something on her mind, but Casey wasn't sure this was really the time for it. If Jenny had questions about her involvement with Colt, he should really be there to help answer them. "Well, I—uh, you know, I really should be getting back to work. It's getting late."

"Okay," Jenny said agreeably, leaving her lunch box on the back step and collecting the hammer and the screwdriver from the grass. "Casey?"

"Yes?" Casey mumbled absently, finally securing the buckle and reaching for the hammer.

"Why don't you have a husband?"

Casey wasn't even aware the wooden handle of the hammer had slipped from her hand until she felt it hit the toe of her boot. "What?"

"A husband," Jenny repeated, reaching for the hammer again. Looking at where it had landed on the toe of Casey's boot, she frowned. "Didn't that hurt?"

"No, it's fine, it's fine," Casey insisted, dismissing the throbbing inside her shoe. "Why do you want to know about that?"

Jenny shrugged, looking up at Casey with wide, innocent eyes. "I don't know. Aunt Mary and Emma said you didn't have one anymore."

"Well, they're right," Casey admitted, taking the hammer again and slipping it through the leather loop on her belt. "I don't."

"Did he go to heaven like my mommy did?"

Casey shook her head. "No, he's fine. He lives in Lake Tahoe now with his new wife." She hesitated for only a fraction of a second. "And new baby."

"He didn't want to be your husband anymore?"

Casey swallowed, marveling at the way children had of getting right to the heart of things. "Something like that."

"So how come you didn't get another one—a husband, I mean?"

"Oh, I don't know," Casey said thoughtfully, taking the screwdriver and slipping it in the ring beside the hammer. "I guess I just never found anyone I cared enough about to want to marry again."

Jenny digested this for a moment. "Daddy doesn't have a wife."

Casey turned and quickly started to walk around the house toward the construction yard. If she hurried, maybe she could get to work before Jenny got too many more questions out. "I know."

"Aunt Mary and Emma think it's time he had one," Jenny added, grabbing for her yellow hard hat on the step and following Casey around the house. "Mostly 'cause of me."

"Oh?" Casey murmured absently, not even wanting to imagine what else Aunt Mary and Emma might be thinking.

"Yeah, they think I need a mother."

Casey reached the yellow line of caution tape marking off the safety zone and ducked underneath it. "What do you think?"

Jenny stopped at the tape, sliding the hard hat on over her curls and watching as Casey continued on. "I think he should marry you."

Casey came to a dead stop. She slowly turned around and stared at Jenny, but couldn't hear anything for a moment because of the loud ringing in her ears. "What?"

"I think Daddy should marry you."

"Whoa," Casey said, shaking her head and walking back to the tape. Ducking beneath it again, she knelt down in front of Jenny. "Slow down here just a minute. Where did that come from? Who's been talking to you about marriage?''

"No one," Jenny insisted.

Casey studied her for a moment, seeing something very curious in her pretty little face. This might not be the most convenient time to talk, but something told her this was too important to put off.

"Okay, young lady," she said, reaching out and giving the hard hat a gentle tap. "Something's going on in that crafty little brain of yours. Might as well 'fess up—tell me what's on your mind."

Jenny dropped her gaze to the ground, swinging her little body back and forth shyly. "I . . . I saw you, the other night, from my window," she confessed. "You and Daddy, when he walked you to the truck."

Casey drew in a deep breath and cursed silently to herself. She remembered Colt's passionate kisses that night and could only imagine the picture the two of them must have made. She hadn't wanted Jenny to find out that way.

"I see," she said with a heavy sigh. "So you saw him kiss me."

Jenny nodded. "He kissed you a lot."

Casey felt the color in her cheeks begin to darken. Colt had indeed kissed her a lot. "How'd you feel about that?"

"Fine," she mumbled, then looked up. "It's just . . ."

"Just what?" Casey prompted when Jenny's words drifted off.

Jenny lifted a shoulder in a small shrug. "They kiss like that in the soaps when they're in love."

Casey had to smile, remembering the small television on the kitchen counter and Emma's interest in a string of daytime dramas. "Yeah, I guess they do."

"And so you and Daddy must be in love, right?"

The innocent bluntness of the question had Casey rocking back on her heels. "Oh, sweetheart," she sighed. "I... I don't know about that. It's not quite the same in real life as it is in the soaps."

"Then what does it mean?"

Casey closed her eyes for a moment. This wasn't going to be easy. Maybe she should have waited until Colt got back. After all, she wasn't exactly experienced in dealing with children, and she wanted to choose her words carefully. "I guess what it means is we've gotten to know each other a little, and we're finding we have certain... feelings for each other. Special feelings."

"Feelings," Jenny repeated.

"That's right," Casey nodded with a smile.

"So it's not love?"

Casey's smile faltered a little. Of course it was love—for her, anyway. She could try to fool Jenny, but there was no use trying to fool herself any longer. She was in love with Colt Wyatt. As a matter of fact, she had to stop herself from taking Jenny by the hand and dancing her around the yard and shouting at the top of her lungs that, yes, she did love her daddy.

But she couldn't do that. How could she? She could only speak for herself. She didn't know what Colt felt. He had told her he wanted her, and every kiss, every touch had made her believe that was true. But when it came to love, she didn't know what was in his heart.

"Sometimes those feelings—those special kinds of feelings are really the beginnings of love. Sometimes they aren't." She stopped for a minute, not sure where to go from there. "Did you talk to your daddy about this?"

Jenny looked away, and she slowly shook her head. "No, I was afraid he'd . . . he'd get mad."

"Because you were watching?"

Jenny nodded. "He says it's not polite to watch people when they don't know it."

"Well, I think he's right about that," she agreed. "But I also think he'd want you to talk to him about anything you have questions about." She reached out and ran a hand along Jenny's golden curls. "I think you should talk to him about all this."

Jenny thought about that for a moment. "Okay, I will."

"Good," Casey said with a smile, quietly breathing a sigh of relief. Hopefully they could drop all this for a while. She patted Jenny on the arm and started to stand.

"Casey?" Jenny said quickly, stopping her with a hand on the arm.

Casey stopped, the smile on her face faltering just a little. "Yes?"

"Do you think those special feelings you and Daddy have are the ones that will turn into love?"

Casey drew in a deep breath and slipped a comforting hand around Jenny's arm. "I don't know, cupcake," she said. "And these things don't just happen overnight. Sometimes it takes a little time to figure out just what's going on." She gave Jenny's arm a small squeeze. "Let's just wait and see what happens, okay?"

"But you are going to get married someday, aren't you?"

"Well, yes, I suppose," she said, considering this for a moment. "I'd like to think I'll get married again—someday."

"And maybe *someday* you'll marry Daddy?"

Casey smiled, but felt her cheeks flush with color. "I think it's a little too early to be talking about marriage." But the smile faded from her lips as she watched Jenny's expression darken and grow troubled. "What's the matter, cupcake?" she asked, giving her arm another squeeze. "You look confused. What don't you understand?"

"Well," Jenny shrugged, giving her head a shake. "Daddy needs a wife, you need a husband, and I need a mommy." She looked up at Casey. "I mean, if you and Daddy got married, wouldn't we all have what we wanted?"

Casey felt her eyes sting with tears, and she quickly blinked them back. "Is . . . is that what you want?"

Jenny nodded, and in a burst of emotion she threw her arms around Casey's neck and hugged tight. "And then you would stay forever and never go away."

Never go away. Jenny's words went off like an air raid siren in her head. Casey didn't want to go away, didn't ever want to leave.

The feel of Jenny's arms hugging her tight had the tears swelling in her eyes and falling down her cheeks. She really couldn't say it yet, couldn't tell Jenny what was in her heart. But the truth was she wanted the same thing. She wanted Colt and Jenny—forever.

"Sure we can't change your mind?"

Colt slipped the thick folder back into his soft-sided briefcase and glanced across the conference table. "I'm sure. I really have to get back."

Joel MacAllister leaned across the table toward him, the golden threads of the Humbolt County Horsemen's Association emblem stitched on the pocket of his blazer gleaming against the afternoon sun. "Come on, the first round's on me. Besides, you deserve it. If that report of yours hadn't been as complete as it was, we'd still be in it up to our eyeballs."

Colt waved off the compliment, but he couldn't help feeling pleased. He had put in many long, hard hours on the report to the state licensing board, and it felt good to have all that work finally pay off. The board had approved their expansion plans and had voted unanimously to issue a show permit for the MLHA. "Thanks, but I'll have to take a rain check. I really do have to be getting back up the hill."

"Sounds important," Joel said. "Dinner date with a lady tonight?"

Colt hesitated, remembering the promise he'd made Casey. He'd agreed to cool it for a while, to take it slow and not to push. "No, no dinner date."

"No? Something a little more than dinner?" Joel hinted with a low chuckle, straightening up. "Come on, don't try and hide it. I know it's a woman. I've got a nose for these things, and buddy you've got all the signs."

Colt only half listened, too distracted by his thoughts and trying to get the zipper of his briefcase to close around the overstuffed file. When he heard everyone around him laughing, he looked up, confused. "Hmm—what? I've got all the what?"

"So who is she?" Joel asked, ignoring his confusion.

"Who's who?" Colt asked.

"The woman who has you heading home for the hills," Joel said, turning to the other board members standing with him. "I mean, come on. What else could it be?"

"What? A woman and the ice man?" joked long-time board member Dale Wilson as he walked up. "No, I don't believe it. Don't tell me some woman has gotten to the last of the stone cold cowboys. What's this world coming to?" He walked up and gave Colt a hearty whack on the shoulder, looking up to the others. "Do you know I've served on just about every breeder's board and organization in the state with this character for the last three years, and all that time he's been telling me he was never going to get seriously entangled with a woman ever again." He gave Colt another slap on the back. "Now don't go telling me some little filly's gone and saddle-broke you."

"Woman," Colt muttered testily, but inwardly he cringed. Was it that obvious? He'd known both Joel and Dale for years, and he knew if they suspected there was a woman in his life, he was in for quite a ribbing. He finished zipping up his briefcase, giving his head a shake. He'd take their ribbing, but he wouldn't have to like it. "I never said anything about a woman."

"You don't have to, we can recognize the signs," Joel pointed out. "You forget—we're all married."

"Something, I might add, I thought you'd sworn off for good," Dale cut in, getting warmed up as the others egged him on. "As a matter of fact, I remember one night after a show up at the Cow Palace in 'Frisco, when this guy here kept me up to the wee hours telling me how no woman was ever going to get her hooks in him again—no siree Bob! This man here was one hombre who wasn't going to let a woman run his life." Dale shook his head, as the others around him guffawed and laughed harder. "No, no, I don't believe it. Tell me he has a mare foaling—I'll believe it. Tell me he's got a stallion that's restless or a sick colt that needs nursing—I'll believe that, too. But a woman?" Dale shook his head. "No, no. Not this boy—he's not the marrying kind."

"'Marrying kind,'" Colt repeated with a disgusted mutter. "What is it with you characters? I barely know the woman, and you've got me married already."

"See, I told you," Joel announced with a loud clap of the hands. "Am I good or what? I knew it was a woman. Why else would any man in his right mind turn down free drinks and a night on the town if it wasn't for a woman? I mean, I know this cowboy. He loves his horses, but not *that* much."

They all hooted, and Dale raised a skeptical brow, shooting Colt a sidelong glance. "Must be some kind of woman."

Some kind of woman. Colt's mind filled with Casey's image—her hair, her eyes, her full, soft lips. He remembered the taste of her, the scent of her, the way she'd felt in his arms. It had been only a little over twelve hours since he'd seen her, and yet already he couldn't wait to see her again.

"You know, she is," he said simply, heading for the door. "She really is."

"Hey, boss lady, come on. It's quittin' time."

Casey looked down through the framed window space and waved to Ronnie and the others in the yard below. "You guys take off. I'm going to stick around here for a while and finish this up."

Watching as they disappeared around the house, she then turned back to the latch on the window seat she was working on. The house was quiet and empty. With Emma having taken Jenny to a birthday party, and Colt not expected back until well after midnight, she had the place to herself. She'd decided to stay and do some work on the window seat, attaching the lid that formed the bench of the seat and enclosed the small storage area beneath.

Casey sank the last screw into the inset hinge, running a gloved finger over the finished brass and inspecting it. There was still a bit of a squeak in it, but she would tend to that later. The important thing now was that they were set right.

Satisfied, she slowly stood up and looked at the small alcove with its bay window and built-in bookshelves, trying to picture how it might look once it was finished and filled with Jenny's stuffed animals and favorite books. Her own private place—that's how Jenny referred to it. And Casey had to admit, some of Jenny's excitement had rubbed off on her, as well. That was why she was staying late, taking extra time and paying special attention. Casey wanted it to be perfect for her.

Casey couldn't help thinking how nice it would be to have a little girl, to plan and design a room for her, filling it with her favorite things. She remembered how Jenny had hugged her this afternoon, how tightly those little arms had squeezed her neck, and a thick knot of emotion formed in her throat. Was it so wrong to want to be part of her life? To want a man and his child?

Casey walked across the room, reached for the drill plug and began winding the long, thick cord slowly around her arm in a loose loop. After her marriage had ended, she had doubted there would ever be anyone in her life again. She wanted a home and a family, but finding someone to care about was a tough job—especially when she spent every minute of her day working.

But that hadn't stopped her from walking into the Wyatt house and finding not only a man to love, but a child to love, as well. What were the odds of that?

She put the drill down with the other tools she'd been using and walked back to the little alcove. She moved the top of the window seat up and down several times, testing the hinges. She was always conscientious about her work, always precise and exact. But this was for Jenny, so she went that extra mile.

She lowered the lid and slid off her work gloves, satisfied it was just how she wanted it, at least for the time being, and sat down on the bench. She looked out the window, trying to imagine Jenny sitting there, looking out across the yard.

Casey remembered the first time Bobby had shown her the blueprints for this project. The first thing she'd noticed had been the design of this small alcove. Bobby had told her the owner of the house had insisted on it—creating the design himself. She remembered being impressed by the design, and by a parent who cared enough to want such a snug, secure place for his child to be. It would have been a place she would have liked for her own little girl—with plenty of light and space and privacy.

There wasn't a doubt in her mind that Colt Wyatt was a wonderful father—the kind of father she would have liked for her own children. He had the kind of patience and understanding that a good parent needed, the kind that came naturally, instinctively, from the heart.

"I'm breaking my promise."

Chapter Nine

Casey jumped at the sound of Colt's voice behind her. Before she knew it, Colt was clutching her to him and pressing his lips onto hers.

Her hands grasped at the front of his shirt, pulling him close. It didn't matter how he'd gotten there—or why. She wasn't thinking about sound, sensible arrangements or the need to take things slow. While the rest of the world spun out of control, she held on tightly to what had become the center of hers—Colt.

"I've been wanting to do that all day," he said against her lips. He reached up and pulled off her hard hat, allowing her long hair to spill free. "I know we agreed, I know I promised to cool it for a while, but..." His words trailed off as he kissed her again.

"You're a terrible man," Casey murmured, feeling breathless and a little dazed.

"I know," he said, pressing small, wet kisses down her neck and along her shoulder. "You're probably angry."

"Furious," she whispered, tilting her head back as his lips made a slow path along her jaw.

"I know, I deserve it," he mumbled, finding her ear and giving the lobe a gentle nibble.

"Yes, you do."

"Are you going to read me the riot act?" he asked, finding her lips again.

"At least," she murmured as he pressed her mouth to his.

Colt felt the desperation growing in his belly, felt his hold beginning to slip. Slowly pulling back, he drew in a deep breath, resting his forehead against hers and willing his heart to stop racing. "Are you really upset?"

Casey smiled, hearing the breathlessness of his words, and tried to control her own uneven breathing. "Do I look upset?"

"No," Colt said with a slow smile. "You look good." He lifted her chin with his finger, bending close for a slow kiss. "Too good, in fact." With another deep breath he set her purposefully away. "And if I don't watch it, I'm going to start breaking a lot of other promises, too."

Casey looked up into his handsome face. It felt good to tease, to joke and just be silly. "I didn't think you were supposed to be back until late tonight."

"I wasn't," he confessed, taking both her hands in his. "And I tried to stay away—I really did." He lifted both her hands to his lips. "But I couldn't." He slowly kissed one finger tip after another. "I missed you too much."

Casey felt her heart swell with emotion in her chest. "I missed you, too."

Colt turned one hand, pressing a kiss into her palm. "So, where is everyone?"

"Gone," she said, thinking how handsome he looked in a sport shirt and slacks. "Emma took Jenny to a birthday party, and the crew took off for the day."

"Oh-oh," Colt groaned, taking her hand and linking their fingers together. "So that means we're alone?"

Casey's eyes narrowed, and she pulled her hands free. "Oh, no you don't," she said, shaking her head and scooting back. "We're not starting that again. Besides, I want to know how it went in Sacramento."

Colt made a careless gesture with his hand, but inwardly his heart swelled. It pleased him to think that she was interested about where he'd been and what he'd done. He told her about the board meeting, about the report he'd filed and the review that had been made. She listened carefully, asking questions and making comments, and he found himself enjoying telling her about his day.

"I'd been all set to debate with them," he said, absently rubbing the back of her hand with the tip of his finger. "Especially on the seating issue. After all, we are a little short of what the state requires, but apparently they were satisfied with the long-term projection I'd prepared." He hesitated for a moment, realizing only then that she was hearing word even before the rest of the MLHA board members. "They went ahead and approved the permit on the first vote and gave us a two-year grace period to get the stadium seating up to code.''

"Oh, Colt," she said, seeing his pleased expression when he told her about the vote. She threw her arms around his neck, hugging him tight, and gave him a kiss on the cheek. "That's wonderful—just *wonderful*. Congratulations.''

Colt felt a strange constricting feeling in his throat, but it had nothing to do with her arms around his neck. He felt overcome with emotion, curiously moved by the suddenness of the hug and spontaneity of her actions. He couldn't seem to explain it, didn't exactly know how or why, but he was strangely touched by the gesture. He would have expected polite interest, maybe a few courteous words and mannerly comments. But there was more than courtesy in her smoky brown eyes. She looked genuinely excited, and it made him feel that she was honestly pleased about the way things had gone today.

Colt realized at that moment that he'd never been in the habit of sharing things with a woman. Oh, he'd shared his bed, but that was a far cry from thoughts and feelings. Karen had never shown an interest in what he felt or what he did. She'd wanted a marriage, and she'd wanted him to support her. Beyond that she'd been so wrapped up in her own problems, in her own life, she'd never taken much of an interest in his. It never would have occurred to her to have asked him about his day.

But then, maybe he hadn't wanted her to.

He looked down into Casey's beautiful face. Everything was so different now. He'd liked coming home, liked the thought of sharing his day with her.

Colt reached out, running a lazy hand through her long, thick hair. There was something so real about her—no pretense, no masquerade. She was genuine, sincere—unselfish with her time and her attention. She'd been happy for him, and that had touched something very deep in him.

"Now let's get back to the part about us being alone," he whispered, edging closer to her on the window seat.

"Oh, no," Casey said, her hands sliding down to his chest and pushing him away. She got up and took a few steps back, shaking her head. "We can't start that again."

"Why not?" he asked in a mischievous voice, following her, backing her against the hard frame of the drywall. "What's wrong with starting again?"

"Nothing," Casey said, feeling him press his body tightly against hers. "It's stopping that gets me worried."

"Then let's not stop," he whispered, lowering his mouth to hers. He marveled at the taste of her and at the desire that pounded inside of him. "Let's never stop."

"Colt, no," Casey pleaded weakly. "No, Colt, we can't." But the appeal sounded weak and hollow even to her own ears, and when his lips touched hers, she did nothing to push him away. The fact was she didn't want to stop, either. She wanted him to kiss her—she wanted him to keep on kissing her until neither one of them could think.

And that just might have happened if it hadn't been for the sounds downstairs. Somewhere through the haze of longing and desire, Casey heard the front door open and the sound of Emma and Jenny talking below.

"Colt," she murmured against his lips. "Colt, it's... it's Jenny. Emma and Jenny—they're home."

Colt slowly reacted, his large body shuddering, and a long sigh leaving his lungs. "Saved by the bell," he whispered in a low growl.

"No thanks to you," she said, pushing out of his arms and stumbling away.

"Oh? I'm suppose to apologize for wanting you?" he asked, watching as she straightened her shirt and ran an uncertain hand through her hair.

She gave him a deliberate look. "No, just for not doing your part."

Colt laughed. "What? I thought I was holding up my end of the deal just fine back there."

Her brown gaze narrowed, doing her best to act annoyed. "That's not what I mean and you know it." She walked to the window seat and picked up her hard hat. "You know," she said, lowering her voice to a stage whisper. "This is never going to work unless you help me."

"You mean this *stopping* business," he concluded dryly, walking up behind her and settling a hand on either hip.

"It's not exactly any easier for me than it is for you," she said, lifting her hair up and attempting to stuff it back inside the hard hat.

"Why, Miss Sullivan," he murmured, placing a light kiss on the exposed part of her neck. "I can't tell you how pleased that makes me feel."

"And I thought we'd agreed," she said, trying her best to ignore the feel of his lips on her. "After all, there's still Jenny to consider."

"Oh, I know. And you're right, we did agree," he conceded, turning her in his arms. He looked down at her, seeing the frustration in her face and loving it. "I just like driving myself crazy, that's all."

Casey glanced up and gave him an exasperated look. "You drive me crazy, too."

"Good," he said, squeezing her tight. "So..." He let his words drift a moment. "What do you say about moving on to the next step."

"The next step?"

"Yeah," he said, trying to keep his tone light despite the fact that he was very, very serious. "It's been three days. Some of the dust has settled. What about moving to—say—a 'date'?"

"A date, huh?" she mused, arching a brow and making a play of considering it. "What did you have in mind?"

"Stay for dinner—with Jenny and me. What do you say?"

Casey smiled, reaching up and giving his cheek a caress. She couldn't think of a more perfect first date. "I say, on to the next step."

Colt smiled, remembering Joel's comment about a date with a beautiful woman. "Come on, let's go down and see Jenny."

"That was fun."

Colt pulled the pink flowered sheet up over Jenny's wiggling body and tucked it under her chin. "What was?"

"Dinner tonight—with Casey."

"Yeah, it was fun," he said with a smile, remembering how he'd completely unnerved Casey by caressing her knee and thigh under the table. He glanced down at Jenny. "You like Casey, don't you?"

"Sure, I like Casey a lot," Jenny said quickly. "You like her, too, don't you?"

Colt reached down and tweaked Jenny's curls. "Yeah, I do." In fact, he was finding it more and more difficult to find anything about the woman he didn't like. "You two have become pretty good friends."

"She's my best friend," Jenny said, pushing the sheet back and struggling to sit up. "Is she your friend, Daddy?"

"Oh, no you don't," Colt said, stopping her with a hand on the shoulder. "I know what you're doing, and it's not going to work."

"What?" Jenny asked innocently.

"Stalling," Colt said firmly. "And it's not going to work. You lie down. You've stayed up too late as it is."

"The sheet's too hot," Jenny complained, wiggling back and forth on the mattress. "And I'm not sleepy."

"You will be," Colt promised. "Once the light is out."

"But I'm not," she insisted, kicking her legs until she was completely free of the sheet. "And I want to talk."

"Talk," Colt sighed, exasperated. It had been a good day, but a long one, and he wanted Jenny in bed asleep so he could relax. Besides, even though Casey had agreed to stay and have dinner with them, they'd had no time alone. Even as she was leaving and he'd walked her out to her truck, Jenny had been with them. There hadn't been so much as an opportunity for a chaste good-night kiss—not exactly what he'd had in mind when he'd suggested the "date." He had managed to whisper to her that he would call her once Jenny had gone to sleep. He lowered himself to the edge of the mattress. "Why is it you always get so chatty at bedtime? We had all evening to talk."

"I don't know." Jenny shrugged, sitting up and tucking her legs beneath her. "I couldn't think of anything to talk about then."

"And now?" Colt asked.

Jenny giggled. "I can think of a lot of things. And Casey says I should talk to you."

Colt paused a moment, the air stalling momentarily in his lungs. "Oh? Well...okay. Five minutes. We'll talk for five minutes and then it's lights out. Got it?"

"I got it," Jenny said with a nod.

"Okay," Colt said, rubbing his hands slowly together. "So what should we talk about? What's on your mind?"

"Marriage."

Colt's hands hesitated, and a chill moved down his spine. Suddenly he wasn't so concerned about the time limit he'd set. He was going to get to the bottom of this no matter how long it took. "Yours or mine?"

"Oh, Daddy," Jenny said, giggling again. "You're such a silly. I'm too little to get married."

"Well, I'm relieved to hear you say that," Colt said dryly, leaning back on the bed. "So what did you want to know about marriage?"

"When are you going to get married again?"

Colt stopped and gave his daughter a deliberate look. "Have you been talking to your Aunt Mary?"

Jenny shook her head. "No, just Casey."

"Casey?" Colt frowned and sat up. "You talked to Casey about marriage?"

"Uh-huh," Jenny said, with a quick nod of her head.

Colt felt a sudden and abrupt interruption in the steady, even rhythm of his heart. "Casey told you to talk to me? About marriage?"

"Yeah," Jenny said. She drew very still, looking up at her father with wide eyes. "And other stuff."

Colt's brow furrowed deeper. "Why were you and Casey talking about marriage?"

Jenny lay back on the pillows and turned on her side, staring at the far wall. "Because... because of what happened the other night."

"The other night?" Colt leaned down and rested a hand on her shoulder. It was only then he realized she wasn't wiggling, wasn't fidgeting about as she usually did. She lay there completely still, and that meant only one thing—this was serious, very serious. "What's the matter, baby?'' he asked, his concern showing in his voice. "What happened the other night?''

"I...I know I was supposed to be asleep, and...and I know it isn't nice to spy, but I wasn't trying to.'' She stopped and turned back around, looking up at him. "Honest.''

"Okay,'' he said in a soothing voice. "It's okay. I believe you. What happened?''

"I—I was looking, and I saw you,'' she said, blurting it out in one long gasp. "I saw you out on the drive with Casey after the barbecue. I saw you kissing her.''

Colt wasn't sure what to do for a moment. He couldn't tell if she was upset or just confused. He reached out, running the backs of his fingers along her soft cheek. Now that he thought of it, she had been a little quiet lately, but he hadn't really thought much about it. Of course, he had been distracted, to say the least. How could he not have seen that Jenny had something on her mind?

"I didn't know, sweetheart, I'm sorry. I wish you would have said something to me sooner instead of keeping it all bottled up,'' he said, looking down into her sweet face and cursing himself for being so blind. "Did it upset you, seeing me kiss her?''

"No,'' Jenny said excitedly, pushing herself up to a sitting position and shaking her head. "I think you should kiss her—a lot!''

Surprise caused him to laugh outright. "Oh, you do, do you? And why's that?''

"So the feelings stuff will turn to love.''

Colt blinked. "Feelings stuff?''

"Yeah, you know—*feelings*," she said again, as though that explained everything.

"Feelings," Colt murmured again, but an uneasy feeling had begun to slowly creep its way through him.

"The special kinds," she said. "Casey said they're the kinds that turn into love."

"Casey said that, huh?" he mumbled, trying his best to follow.

"Yeah," Jenny said, her enthusiasm growing. "And she says, you know, when they're over and it's love, you can get married."

"Married?" Colt repeated, feeling the gooseflesh along his arm start to rise. "To Casey."

"Right," Jenny said. With all the secrets out, she was feeling much better, and she looked up at her father and grinned.

"That's what Casey wanted you to talk to me about?"

"Yeah," Jenny said again, rising up on her feet and jumping up and down. "Special feelings and love and us all having what we want."

Colt watched Jenny bounding up and down for a moment, cautioning himself not to jump to conclusions, not to let his imagination—or his suspicions—get out of hand. But why would Casey put Jenny up to something like this?

"Sit down here," Colt said, suspicion making him testy. He reached up, grabbing Jenny's arm, and settled her down on the bed beside him again. "Let me get this straight. You think because I kissed Casey that I'll marry her now?"

"After, you know, after the special feeling stuff turns—"

"I know, I know, turns to love," he said impatiently, finishing for her. "Casey told you that?"

Jenny nodded her head and wiggled out of his hold. "And tonight it was almost like we were a family already, wasn't it?" she said, slipping back under the sheet. "You and me and Casey and Emma."

Colt barely heard Jenny, wasn't even aware that she'd slid from under his arm and crawled back beneath the sheet. "Are you sure Casey said you should talk to me about marriage?"

"Uh-huh," Jenny said, settling her head just right on the pillow and stifling a yawn. "'Cause then she'll be with us forever and never go away." She reached up and pulled Colt close for a hug. "If you and Casey would just get married, we'd all get what we want."

Colt leaned down and gave his daughter a goodnight kiss. Lifting himself off the mattress, he headed for the door, leaving it open a crack just as she liked it, so the hall light would shine inside.

He made his way down the hall, passing the area where the new wing joined the existing hall and past the open doorway into Jenny's unfinished bedroom.

He stepped inside, walking through the darkness to the window seat. He stared out through the open window frame into the hot, black night. He had sat here with Casey just a few short hours before.

Marriage. Why would Casey have told Jenny to talk to him about marriage? Why wouldn't she have brought the subject up herself?

He sat down on the window seat, looking up at the stars and thinking about how happy he'd felt sitting there with her. He'd felt like coming home this time had really been *coming home*.

So what was it that bothered him—the mention of marriage? It wasn't like the subject hadn't crossed his mind once or twice in the past several days, because it had. Ever since that night at the pond, he'd fantasized about what it might be like if the two of them were to get married. Was it so unreasonable to assume she might have had some thoughts about that herself? Shouldn't that have pleased him, shouldn't that have made him feel better?

So why didn't it?

Casey says I should talk to you. Jenny's words sounded over and over again in his head, turning his blood cold and the knot in his stomach rock hard. It was Casey who'd been concerned about Jenny in the first place, who'd wanted to take it slowly, to ease her into things gently and carefully. Why would she have wanted to involve Jenny now?

Colt lifted himself off the window seat, running a hand over the wood bench and marveling at Casey's handiwork. She was a perfectionist with a real eye for detail.

He turned and walked back through the unfinished room to the hall. What detail had she been seeing to when she'd talked with Jenny? What plan was she following that required his daughter's help to carry out?

Casey pulled the pickup to a stop behind Ronnie's old station wagon and Jake's truck. She'd been re-

lieved to see them when she'd pulled into the drive. At
least they'd made it to work on time.

Casey turned off the ignition. Her head ached.
She'd awakened feeling as if a thick fog had settled
around her, and things hadn't improved much since.
She leaned across the seat, reaching for the thermos of
coffee she'd filled at a convenience store. She was
tempted not to even bother with the cup, just open the
screw stopper and down the contents in one gulp. She
needed caffeine—and a lot of it.

Why had she stayed up so late? She should have just
gone to bed as she always did and let the phone wake
her up. But she hadn't. Foolishly she'd remained up
half the night waiting...waiting for Colt to call.

She turned and looked up at the house. It was almost the middle of the morning. No doubt he'd be
up—fresh and well rested. And why shouldn't he be?
He hadn't waited up half the night for a call that had
never come.

Casey closed her eyes, feeling a dull, painful throb
at her temples. Of course, it was her own fault. No one
had forced her to wait up—she'd known then it was a
stupid thing to do. And yet she'd done it, anyway—sat
there and waited like a wallflower waiting for a dance.

But this wasn't about a school dance. She and Colt
weren't teenagers any longer. They were both adults,
should both be well beyond the age of playing games.
When a person tells another person they'll call, they
should call. He'd called her before when he'd said he
would, so why hadn't he called her last night?

Casey rubbed her temples, swearing quietly under
her breath and thinking what a pathetic picture she

must have made, waiting by the phone. She hadn't been too concerned when ten o'clock had come and gone. After all, it had been nearly nine when she'd left the ranch last night. He'd had to get Jenny in bed, get her settled down. And even when it got to be eleven, she still hadn't been concerned. She'd told herself he'd probably fallen asleep reading Jenny a bedtime story. She'd even pictured him in her head, sitting up with his head slouched to one side, waking up with a stiff neck and feeling confused. But then eleven-thirty had come, and then midnight, one, two. She'd been so annoyed by that time it hadn't mattered how tired she'd felt, she'd been too stirred up to sleep.

It was after three when she'd finally drifted off, and then she'd slept the sleep of the dead, missing her six o'clock alarm completely. She'd finally woken up around eight, feeling dull and confused, and even the cold shower she'd taken and the mad dash to work hadn't helped.

She walked to the back of her pickup, reaching into one of the two huge built-in toolboxes to find her hard hat and tool belt. She gathered them carelessly in one arm, carrying her thermos in the other, and started down the drive.

She looked around, expecting Colt to appear at any moment. What was she supposed to say to him now? Rant and rave and demand to know why he hadn't called? Or was she just supposed to forget it—pretend it had never happened.

She wanted to be mad. He'd said he would call, and he hadn't, and the long and the short of it was it had hurt her feelings. But still, it was just a phone call. As transgressions go, it was a small one. It wasn't as if he'd kept her waiting at the altar or anything like that. And as nice as it would be to have someone to blame for a lost night's sleep, the fact remained that no one had held a gun to her head last night, forcing her to wait up. She had no one to blame but herself.

Rounding the corner of the house, she spotted Ronnie and Jake working on the second story. She gave them a wave, relieved they were too busy with finishing up the drywall in Jenny's new room to have time to rib her about being late.

She stopped at the back porch, setting her thermos on the step and slipping the tool belt around her waist. Securing the buckle tight, she reached for the thermos and unscrewed the plastic cup from the top.

Just smelling the coffee made her feel better. She filled the cup, taking time to savor the aroma again before gingerly taking a sip.

"I thought you'd decided to take the day off."

Chapter Ten

Casey looked up through the screen on the porch and gave Colt a smile. She forgot about being mad, about her sleepless night and her hurt feelings. Just seeing him made her feel better.

"No, I wouldn't dare," she said, giving her head a shake. "The boss on this job would fire me for sure." But the smile on her face faltered when he pushed the screen open and she looked up into his eyes. Something was wrong. He didn't need to say anything, and she didn't need to ask. It was written all over his face. "Colt, what is it? Is Jenny all right?"

Colt walked down the steps, letting the screen bang closed behind him. "Jenny's fine. Why?"

Casey gave her head a small shake. "No reason, you just looked so..."

"So...what?" he demanded when her words trailed off.

She looked up at him, surprised by the harshness of his voice. "I don't know," she said, her own voice rising a degree. She felt herself getting defensive, but she had no clue as to why, or what about. "Troubled, I guess. Or angry."

"Angry? Why should I be angry?"

Casey stared up at him for a moment, taking a deep breath, feeling bewildered and confused. "Colt. What's this all about? What's happened?"

Colt hesitated for a moment. He didn't even feel the fatigue of his sleepless night, or the strain of endless hours spent pacing the small length of his room. He was too pumped up right now—his system too flooded with adrenaline to feel much of anything at all.

"Jenny talked to me last night," he said, watching her closely. "As a matter of fact, we had a nice long chat."

He waited for a reaction, some sign that she understood the significance of what he'd just said. He wanted her to know that he knew—he *knew*. He was onto her, he knew she'd used Jenny to try to get what she wanted.

Of course, he wasn't exactly sure how he'd envisioned her exactly—looking guilty maybe, gasping in horror, denying everything, tossing herself at his feet with a full-blown confession of some sort. But none of that happened. She never even batted an eye. She stood and looked at him guiltlessly.

"Well," she said with a small laugh, feeling almost as relieved as she did foolish. She should have known

it was something like that—after all, Jenny had had
questions about seeing them together. It was good that
they'd talked about it. Casey's smile widened, picturing father and daughter sitting together on her bed,
talking late into the night. "That explains it, then."

His blue gaze narrowed. He couldn't believe it. She
was as cool as a cucumber. "Then maybe you
wouldn't mind explaining it to me."

"Me!" she blurted out with a teasing laugh, flipping her hair around her hand and tucking it into her
hard hat. "What explaining do I have to do? In case
you've forgotten, my friend, you're the one who didn't
call last night."

He looked into her dark brown eyes. She was right,
of course, he hadn't called. But the answers he wanted
from her should come face-to-face, not over a telephone line.

He'd felt shell-shocked last night. Nothing Jenny
had told him made sense. He knew Casey would be
waiting for his call, but he hadn't been ready to talk
yet. Instead, he'd gone down to the stables and hitched
Snapper to the buggy, taking the same familiar path
out to the pond.

He'd needed time to think, time to clear his mind.
But the quiet pond, the moon and the stars did little to
help. He'd only felt more confused and restless. All
he'd been able to think about was being there with
Casey, and wanting her more than he'd ever wanted
anything in his life.

But had their night at the pond been real? Had the
emotions and the desires that had passed between
them really been there, or had they just been some

artfully crafted design, just part of a grander scheme she'd fashioned from the beginning?

Those questions had nagged at him for the rest of the night—turning around in his head, torturing him, tormenting him. And now he wanted answers.

"You're right," he said, taking a step closer, trying not to look at her lips and remember how they had tasted. "I didn't, because I thought we should talk face-to-face."

Casey's hand paused as she tucked at her hair. She regarded him carefully, seeing the cold, unemotional look in his eyes and feeling a shiver travel the length of her spine.

"Okay," she murmured, slipping the hat off and tossing it onto the step, letting her hair tumble free. "Face-to-face, let's talk."

"Like I said, Jenny talked to me last night," he said, taking a step closer. "She said you'd told her to."

Casey thought back to the conversation she and Jenny had had the day before. "Yes, I guess I did."

"You *guess* you did?" he demanded, his voice booming louder than he'd intended. "Are you saying Jenny's lying?"

Casey stared up at him, hardly knowing how to respond. What had happened to him, what kind of strange metamorphosis had taken place? She felt as though she'd awakened into someone else's life—not entirely sure how she got there or what to do.

"No," Casey said, balling her hands into fists and settling them defensively at her hips. "How could you even say something as preposterous as that?"

"How could you be so presumptuous as to ask my daughter to do your bidding?"

"Do my *bidding*?" Casey repeated in disbelief, hardly believing what it was she was hearing. "Have you lost your mind? I made a simple suggestion."

"Oh, is that what you call it, a suggestion?"

"You wouldn't?"

"Damn straight I wouldn't." He laughed—a harsh, grating sound. "I'd call it what it is—exploitation, manipulation—"

"Manip—" Casey's voice broke with shock and surprise, and she felt a strange, tingling sensation in her arms and legs. "I don't believe this. You're talking crazy."

"What's crazy is getting a child to do your dirty work for you."

"My dirty work," she repeated, shaking her head. This all seemed so ridiculous, so unreal she could hardly believe it was happening. She thought back to that silly cupcake she had given Jenny all those weeks ago and how upset he'd gotten over that. Was that all this was—him overreacting again?

"Look, Colt," she said in as calm a voice as she could manage. "Jenny had some concerns because she saw us together in the driveway the other night. I encouraged her to talk to you about it—that's all. That's all there was to it."

"Oh, right," he scoffed. "And I suppose the part about you and me getting married was all Jenny's idea?"

"What?"

"You and Jenny didn't talk about marriage?"

"Well . . . yes, we did, but—"

"There," he said, gesturing like a lawyer in court. "You admit it." He took a step closer, looking down into her eyes and feeling the muscles in his chest seize tight. There was such emotion in her eyes, such feeling that he cursed, hating himself for wanting her despite the anger raging in his heart. "Casey, if you wanted to know if I was interested in marrying you, why didn't you just come to me yourself? Why did you use Jenny? Why did you get her involved?"

"You think I asked Jenny to talk to you about marriage?" Casey asked, choking out the words. She stared at him, shaking her head incredulously. "I don't believe it. I don't believe that's what she told you."

"She didn't have to," he snorted. "I could see what was going on." He reached out, grabbing Casey by the upper arm. "Where was all that concern you had for Jenny when you were using her to talk me into marriage? What happened to going slow for her sake, to not wanting her upset or frightening her? Didn't that apply to marriage—or just sleeping with me?"

Casey felt a cold, deadly calm move through her. She carefully and purposefully pulled out of his hold, looking up into the face of a man she didn't know at all. "You *jerk.*"

The calm, unemotional remark surprised him, bringing him up short. "What?"

"You heard me," she said, her voice low and cold. "I don't believe you. What kind of conceited, egomaniac are you, anyway?" But she didn't wait for him to answer, charging on instead. "What do you think you are, some kind of *prize,* God's gift to women, so sought after that a woman would do anything, use anyone she could for the *privilege* of wearing your ring on her finger?"

"You're not the first woman who's used Jenny to get something from me," he said, striking back.

She marched up to him, glaring into his icy blue eyes. "Well, Colton Wyatt, you self-centered, narcissistic cretin. You can relax. There isn't anything I want from you. As a matter of fact, I wouldn't have you if you came wrapped in a basket like a Christmas goose." Anger felt good in her veins, like a potent drug that dulled the pain of being unjustly accused. "You know, you don't deserve a wonderful little girl like Jenny. She deserves someone in her life who knows about love, who knows about giving and sharing. Not some uptight, self-important creep who's so afraid of showing any real emotion that he has to invent excuses to push people away." She snatched her hat up from the step, turned and started back for the truck. "Goodbye, Colt."

"But I don't understand," Jenny sobbed, tears streaming down her cheeks. "I don't want you to go."

Casey blinked, her own eyes smarting with tears. But she had to hold on—for Jenny's sake as well as her own. "I know sweetheart. I know."

The little girl had obviously witnessed the heated exchange between her and Colt. She had charged outside after Colt's departure, tears streaming down her face. "But . . . but you said you and Daddy had feelings," Jenny wept. "Weren't they the special kind, the kind that turn to love?"

Casey squeezed her eyes tight, pulling Jenny into her arms. "I guess not, baby." She looked down into her tear-filled eyes. "But that doesn't mean you and I still can't be friends. We can talk on the phone—as often as you want. And I'll talk to your daddy about a visit now and then, too."

But Jenny merely sobbed harder. "It won't be the same," she moaned, shaking her head back and forth. "It—it won't be the same ever again."

Casey wanted to argue with her, wanted to soothe away her tears and tell her everything was going to be all right, but she couldn't. It wasn't the same—it would never be the same again. Colt had accused her of using Jenny, of manipulating and exploiting a child. He couldn't know her, couldn't begin to care, and accuse her of such a thing. It was over. Everything was over.

"I've got to go now," Casey whispered, reaching down and wiping at the tears on Jenny's cheek.

"No," Jenny pleaded, sobbing harder. "No, please don't go."

Casey closed her eyes, not sure she had the strength to do what needed to be done. Taking a deep breath, she rose slowly to her feet, setting Jenny away from her. "Don't cry now, sweetheart, please. I'll call you tonight, check and make sure everything is all right? Okay?"

Jenny nodded her head, but nothing could stop the tears. Casey headed down the drive to her truck, seeing Jenny in the rearview mirror and feeling the hold on her own emotions start to give way. By the time she'd reached the road, her vision was clouded and blurred by the tears.

"Damn you, Colt Wyatt," she murmured, steering blindly down the deserted road. "Damn you."

The warble of the telephone shattered the quiet night like an air raid siren blasting out a warning. Even though Casey had been wide awake, the unexpected sound brought her heart to her throat and left her feeling confused and disoriented. She fumbled for the telephone on the nightstand, trying to think what crisis had occurred at what job site and what she was going to do to fix it.

"H-hello?" she said, reading 2:47 a.m. on the clock beside the bed.

"If you're hiding her, for God's sake tell me. This isn't going to help solve anything."

It had been almost a week since Casey had heard Colt's voice, and she barely recognized it now. Bobby had taken over for her at the job site. She'd been grateful that he'd simply done what she'd asked, forgoing any questions he might have had. After all, she'd never asked him to finish up a job for her before. She'd spent the past five days concentrating on several new jobs that were in the works, and trying desperately not to think about Colt Wyatt. Jenny had called her several times during the week, but they'd been tearful conversations and difficult for them both.

But Colt's voice over the line wasn't angry, it was desperate. "Colt? Wh-what is it? What did you say?"

"Jenny. Tell me you have her. Tell me she's there with you."

"Jenny?" Casey sat straight up in bed. "What are you talking about? Jenny's not here."

"You don't have her? She didn't come to you?"

"Colt, what are you talking about?" Casey demanded, sliding her feet to the floor and sitting on the edge of the bed. "Why would you think she was here? Where is she?"

For a moment there was only silence on the line, and when he did speak, it was with a very different voice. "She's gone."

"Gone?" All the feeling left her hands, and she could barely hear his voice for the ringing in her ears. "And you thought I took her?"

"No, I—I thought—" There was an abrupt silence, and it took a moment for him to speak again. "I thought she'd go to you. I—I don't know where she is, Casey. My baby's gone."

Casey not only heard the sound of pain in his voice, she heard desperation. Colt Wyatt was a broken man. "I'll be right there."

She really had no conscious recollection of having gotten dressed or climbing into her truck and traveling the three miles over country roads that took her from her small apartment to the Cache Creek Ranch, but somehow she'd managed to do both. From the road, Casey could see the porch light, glowing yellow in the distance, but fear consumed her when she pulled into the drive and saw the cluster of blue-and-white units from the Calavaras County Sheriff's Office.

She pulled to a stop behind one of the squad cars. Racing up the walk, she headed for the cluster of people gathered on the porch. But before she could reach them, Colt was there, running toward her.

"Casey." He reached out and took her outstretched hands.

"Did you find her?" she gasped, feeling breathless and desperate. "Do you know where she is?" She looked around at the uniformed officers and started to tremble. "What are they doing here?"

"They're organizing a search," Colt said, in a voice that was too calm, too unemotional to be natural. But when he looked down into her fear-stricken face, he felt the fragile hold on his own emotions start to slip. "I didn't know what else to do. I went in to check on her on my way up to my room. Her bed was empty." He squeezed his eyes tight, taking a deep breath, then looked into her eyes again. "Casey, we've looked everywhere. I don't know where she is."

"Colt," Casey whispered in a rush, gathering him up in her arms without hesitation. This wasn't the time for anger and recriminations. Jenny—the child they both loved—was missing, and at that moment nothing else mattered.

"It's my fault—all my fault." His voice choked against the silky softness of her hair, thick and raw with emotion. "She's been so upset the past few days—wouldn't talk, wouldn't eat. I couldn't stand it anymore. I tried to get her to talk to me, tried to get her to cry—to do *something*." He shook his head, taking a deep breath. "It ended in a terrible quarrel, she got angry. She told me she'd heard you and me arguing that day. Told me that... I'd messed everything up and it was my fault that you'd left. She blamed me for taking you from her, for sending you away." He stopped, struggling against a wave of despair. He pulled back, looking down into Casey's tear-filled eyes. "She hates me, Casey. She said she wanted to run away and live with you and never come back again." He stopped, his eyes bright with tears he wouldn't let fall. "I feel so helpless. I feel so damn helpless."

"Colt," she whispered, looking up into his eyes and feeling his pain in her own heart. "Colt, you know she didn't mean that. Jenny loves you—you mean everything to her. We're going to find her. Do you hear me? We're going to find her and bring her home."

Colt held on to her words like a lifeline. He didn't question why they'd meant so much, or why he felt better just having her near. The important thing was that they both loved Jenny and wanted her back.

The search started with the ranch and then spread out to the countryside surrounding it. Colt and Casey both went out with the various search teams, as did Mac and Sid Wyatt, canvassing the area and inspecting every rock, every stream and every valley in a five-mile radius of the house. But the terrain was rugged, and the long night took its toll on everyone. Colt returned to the house just before daybreak, finding that Casey had just returned ahead of him. She sat at the kitchen table with Emma and his Aunt Mary, looking drained and exhausted. When he walked into the room, all three women rose to their feet.

"Nothing yet," he said, shaking his head in response to their unspoken question. "The teams are regrouping and we'll head back out after daylight."

"Sit here," Emma said, indicating a chair at the table as she walked to the stove. She poured a mug of coffee and carried it back to the table, setting it down in front of him. "You look like you're ready to drop."

"I'm fine," Colt insisted, his gaze turning to Casey. "You okay?"

"Fine," Casey lied, nodding her head. She didn't want to tell him how she really felt, how scared and frightened. She didn't want to think about it herself. It was better to just sit there and pretend everything was going to be all right when she really was terrified.

"Is Sid back?" Mary Wyatt asked, her eyes red and swollen from crying.

Colt shook his head. "He went up with the crew searching the…" Emotion choked in his throat and he rubbed his eyes. "They're … uh … searching the pond."

Casey felt her eyes burn with tears, but she blinked them quickly away. Everyone was silent, too lost in their own desperate thoughts to know what to say or what to do. Casey couldn't remember ever having felt so frustrated or so impatient—as if she was about ready to scream. The search had been exhausting, groping about in the dark, but at least she'd felt like she was doing *something*. Just sitting was driving her crazy.

"Did she say anything last night?" Casey finally asked, not able to take the awful silence any longer.

Colt looked at her from across the table, seeing the dark circles below her eyes and realizing at that moment that she loved Jenny—probably as much as he did. "No," he said, shaking his head, dropping his gaze to the butcher block table and trying not to think of how upset Jenny had been, or how angry. "She just kept saying she was going to run away, that she didn't want her new bed or her new room—nothing."

Casey thought for a moment. As hard as she tried, she couldn't imagine Jenny telling her father she wanted to run away. Jenny would have gotten mad, she would have fussed and pouted, threatened not to sit on his lap or not kiss him good-night—but run away? Where would she even have gotten the idea? Jenny loved her father, she loved her home and the ranch, she loved Emma and her Great-Uncle Sid and Aunt Mary, she loved Mac and Mountain Lady and Snapper and rides in the buggy. Cache Creek Ranch was her whole life, she would never want to leave everything she loved—not for any reason.

"Colt," Casey said after a moment. "Did Jenny ever actually say she wanted to run away—I mean, literally use those words?"

"Yes," Colt said, looking up from the table and nodding his head—but stopped abruptly. "Well, I mean...I don't know exactly. She said something like she didn't want to be here anymore. That she wanted to be with you—with Casey in your own secluded place."

"Oh, my God," Casey gasped, leaping up from her chair so fast it toppled backward behind her.

"Casey, wait," Colt called after her as she rounded the table and ran toward the stairs. He caught her halfway up the steps. "Casey, what it is? Where are you going?"

"Colt, oh, Colt, don't you get it?" she said, her voice edging on the sane side of hysterical. "Don't you remember? Her private place. She wanted her own—"

"—*private place,*" Colt finished for her. There was a moment—a clear, brilliant, crystallized moment when they both knew what the other was thinking— and they both knew they were right.

Then, as though responding to the same, silent command, they turned and raced up the steps together, leaving Emma and Mary standing at the bottom with eyes wide and mouths hanging open.

"*Jenny!*" Colt shouted, running down the hall toward her half-finished room.

"*Jenny,*" Casey called out at the same time.

The faint rays of the morning sun peeked through the bay window, lending just enough light for them to find their way through the room. At the window seat, Colt reached around Casey and lifted the lid.

The hinges squeaked, and somewhere in the back of Casey's mind she told herself she would find a way to fix that. But then the thought disappeared from her head completely, for suddenly it was as though the small window seat had become a treasure chest—containing the most valuable cache of all.

Nestled on a blanket, surrounded by a company of colorful stuffed animals stationed around her like sentries on guard, and her tool belt and hard hat, Jenny stirred sleepily. She rubbed at her eyes, peering through heavy lids. "Daddy?"

"Yes, sweetheart," he said, reaching down and gathering her up in his arms. "It's Daddy."

She slipped her arms around his neck as he slowly stood up, resting a cheek on his shoulder. Spotting Casey in the dim light, her eyes opened wider. "Casey?"

"Good morning, cupcake," Casey said, rising up on tiptoe and giving her a kiss on the cheek. "You gave us all quite a scare."

Jenny reached out, curling a lock of Casey's hair around her hand. "Is it all better now, Casey? Is it love yet?"

But Casey never had a chance to answer. Emma burst into the room out of breath, her face flushed.

"Lord in heaven," she gasped, coming to a dead stop at the door.

"I don't believe it," Mary Wyatt cried, tears streaming down her face as she peered over Emma's shoulder. "They're never going to believe this at the next MLHA board meeting."

For Casey the next two hours were as hectic and as confusing as any she'd spent in her life. Colt had done his best to give Jenny a stern lecture, but it had been a little hard when he'd been so obviously glad to see her. Needless to say, everyone involved with the search was elated that Jenny had been found safe. It didn't seem to matter that there'd been a long night of searching, that Jenny had been snug in her own home the whole time—not when it meant that a child was safe.

It took a while for the hoopla to die down, for reports to be made and the search to be called off. But eventually people began to leave, the squad cars pulled from the driveway and the phone finally stopped ringing. Casey's head throbbed, and her whole body ached from a night of strain and worry.

She looked about, but Colt was nowhere in sight. It was just as well. She wasn't sure she could handle another farewell scene with him. She wanted to just slip out—get away before anyone noticed.

"Well, I'm going home," she said to Jenny, who sat beside her at the kitchen table, eating a bowl of corn flakes. "I need a shower and a few hours of sleep."

"Will you be coming back?"

Casey smiled down at Jenny, reaching across the table and putting a hand on hers. "Maybe a little later. I'll call you, okay?"

"Casey?" Jenny said, stopping her as she started to rise. "It's not love yet, is it?"

"It is for me."

Casey and Jenny both turned at the sound of the deep voice behind them. Colt stood in the arch of the breakfast nook, smiling at them with a grin that stretched from ear to ear.

"Is it, Daddy?" Jenny asked, leaping off the chair and running to her father. "Is it really?"

Colt picked his daughter up in his arms, hiking her up on his hip. He turned, looking across the small room to Casey.

"I can't ask you to forgive me," he said to Casey, taking the few short steps needed to bring them together. "What I did—the things I said, they're unforgivable. I can only say I'd let what happened in the past get in the way of what I feel now." He reached out, running the backs of his fingers along her cheek. "But I love you."

"Colt, please," Casey whispered. "This really isn't the time. We're all exhausted, last night—"

"Last night I had nothing," he said, cutting her off, ignoring her protest. "I never thought I'd have a chance to make up for all the stupid things I'd done." He paused for a moment, looking down into her soft brown eyes and knowing he would never love her more than he did at this moment. "Casey, I've been given a second chance. I'm through making mistakes, I'm through running scared. I don't want to 'take it slow,' I want to grab on to what I have while I can. If I learned anything last night, it was not to assume anything. In the wink of an eye it can all disappear, and I don't want to risk losing everything again. I love you, Casey. Jenny loves you."

"I do," Jenny said, chiming in. "Yes, I do."

"Love me," he whispered, slipping his free arm around her waist and pulling her close. "Marry me?"

"Marry us," Jenny corrected, reaching a hand out and stroking Casey's hair. "Please?"

Casey forgot about her headache; the ringing in her ears made it all but impossible for her to think of anything else. She looked up at Colt, then to Jenny and then back to Colt again. "I . . . I don't know what to say."

"Say yes," he murmured, pressing a soft kiss against her mouth. He felt the resistance in her body, but he wasn't about to give up. "I know I've made mistakes, but it's no mistake that I love you, and that's never going to change. Marry me—" His gaze flicked to his daughter for an instant, and he smiled. "Marry us. Say yes, and we'll all have what we want."

Casey didn't realize she was crying until she felt the tears run down her cheeks. In the last few hours she'd been on an emotional roller coaster, plummeting to the depths of fear and despair and soaring to the heights of happiness—but this, this was too much. She knew she should take some time, knew she should weigh the issues and consider the risks. It wasn't just her heart—she wanted to do what was best for all of them.

But looking up at Colt and Jenny, their blue eyes bright and expectant, she realized none of those things mattered. They were details, mere technicalities to be worked out later. All that was really important was that they were together, and together they were happy.

Feeling a little like the roller coaster ride had only just begun, Casey looked up at them and smiled. "Yes."

Epilogue

"Anybody home?"

Casey felt her heart skip a beat. "We're up here."

"Brrr, it's cold out there," Colt called out as he made his way up the stairs and down the hall toward Jenny's bedroom. He stopped just inside the door, looking across the room at the two of them sitting together on the window seat, and forgetting about the frigid wind howling outside. "You two look cozy."

"We are," Jenny said, flipping a page of the book she held and nestling deeper under the old-fashioned quilt that covered them both. "Can we decorate the Christmas tree tonight?"

"Okay with me," he said, turning to Casey and making his way across the room. "How are you doing? That flu of yours any better?"

"Yes," Casey said in a small voice, exchanging a quick look with Jenny. "I'm fine."

"Think you're going to feel up to trimming the tree tonight?" he asked, bending down and planting a quick kiss on her lips.

"Sure. I'd love it," she said, scooting to one side to make room for him.

"We can wait, if you want," he assured her, lowering himself onto the seat beside her. His hand found hers, his fingers absently twirling the gold band he'd slipped on her finger four months before. "If you're not feeling up to it."

"No, I'm fine, really," she assured him. She and Jenny looked at each other and smiled.

"What?" he asked slowly, eyeing the two of them suspiciously. "What was all that about?"

"What was what?" Jenny asked innocently, but she looked up at Casey again and grinned widely.

"That," Colt said, pointing a finger. "What's up with you two?"

"Nothing," Casey said with a small laugh, giving his hand a squeeze. "I swear, you're getting paranoid."

"Yeah? Well if I am, it comes from living in a houseful of females," he said dryly. "What we need is some more male blood around here."

Jenny coughed out another giggle, covering her mouth with both hands.

Colt's lids narrowed. "All right, that's it. What's going on? What's happened?"

"Nothing," Casey insisted, but she couldn't help smiling herself. The happiness was just too much, too much to keep inside. "I was just thinking about an idea I had for another addition."

"Oh, no," Colt groaned, shaking his head definitely. "Casey, we've just got this place put back together. No more construction—please."

"Well I was just thinking," she mused. "If I knocked a wall out in the room next door where the extra closet is, I could put one of those loft beds in the alcove. You know—the ones with the ladder to climb up and the pole to slide down?"

"A loft bed," Colt repeated incredulously. "What would we want a loft bed in the spare room for?"

"For my little brother," Jenny said in a burst of laughter.

"Brother?" Colt looked at Casey, seeing the tears in her eyes. "A . . . a baby?"

She looked up at him, putting a hand to his cheek. "Sometime in August. Is that enough male blood for you?"

He gathered her into his arms, kissing her long and deep. "Just what I want."

*   *   *   *   *

Silhouette®

AVAILABLE THIS MONTH FROM SILHOUETTE ROMANCE®

#1198 MAD FOR THE DAD
Terry Essig

#1199 HAVING GABRIEL'S BABY
Kristin Morgan

#1200 NEW YEAR'S WIFE
Linda Varner

#1201 FAMILY ADDITION
Rebecca Daniels

#1202 ABOUT THAT KISS
Jayne Addison

#1203 GROOM ON THE LOOSE
Christine Scott

Take 4 bestselling love stories FREE

Plus get a FREE surprise gift!

Special Limited-time Offer

Mail to Silhouette Reader Service™

3010 Walden Avenue
P.O. Box 1867
Buffalo, N.Y. 14240-1867

YES! Please send me 4 free Silhouette Romance™ novels and my free surprise gift. Then send me 6 brand-new novels every month, which I will receive months before they appear in bookstores. Bill me at the low price of $2.67 each plus 25¢ delivery and applicable sales tax, if any.* That's the complete price and a savings of over 10% off the cover prices—quite a bargain! I understand that accepting the books and gift places me under no obligation ever to buy any books. I can always return a shipment and cancel at any time. Even if I never buy another book from Silhouette, the 4 free books and the surprise gift are mine to keep forever.

215 BPA A3UT

Name	(PLEASE PRINT)	
Address	Apt. No.	
City	State	Zip

This offer is limited to one order per household and not valid to present Silhouette Romance™ subscribers. *Terms and prices are subject to change without notice. Sales tax applicable in N.Y.

USROM-898   ©1990 Harlequin Enterprises Limited

Five irresistible men say "I do" for a lifetime of love
in these lovable novels—our Valentine to you in February!

I'M YOUR
GROOM

#1205 *It's Raining Grooms* by Carolyn Zane
After praying every night for a husband, Prudence was suddenly
engaged—to the last man she'd ever expect to marry!

#1206 *To Wed Again?* by DeAnna Talcott
Once Mr. and Mrs., Meredith and Rowe Worth were now adoptive
parents to a little girl. And blessed with a second chance at marriage!

#1207 *An Accidental Marriage* by Judith Janeway
Best man Ryan Holt never wanted to be a groom himself—until a
cover-up left everyone thinking he was married to maid of honor
Kit Kendrick!

#1208 *Husband Next Door* by Anne Ha
When Shelly got engaged to a stable, *boring* fiancé, her neighbor and
very confirmed bachelor Aaron Carpenter suddenly realized *he* was
meant to be her husband!

#1209 *Wedding Rings and Baby Things* by Teresa Southwick
To avoid scandal, very pregnant Kelly Walker needed a husband fast,
not forever. But after becoming Mrs. Mike Cameron, Kelly fell for this
father figure!

Don't miss these five wonderful books,
Available in February 1997,
only from

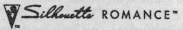

Silhouette ROMANCE™

Look us up on-line at: http://www.romance.net   SR-GROOM

He's able to change a diaper in three seconds flat.
And melt an unsuspecting heart even more quickly.
But changing his mind about marriage might take some doing!
He's more than a man...
He's a FABULOUS FATHER!

***

January:
MAD FOR THE DAD by Terry Essig (#1198)
Daniel Van Scott asked Rachel Gatlin for advice on raising his nephew—
and soon noticed her charms as both a mother...*and* a woman.

February:
DADDY BY DECISION by Lindsay Longford (#1204)
Rancher Jonas Riley proposed marriage to Jessica McDonald! But
would Jonas still want her when he found out a secret about her
little boy?

March:
MYSTERY MAN by Diana Palmer (#1210)
50th Fabulous Father! Tycoon Canton Rourke was a man of mystery,
but could the beautiful Janine Curtis find his answers with a lifetime
of love?

May:
MY BABY, YOUR SON by Anne Peters (#1222)
Beautiful April Bingham was determined to reclaim her long-lost child.
Could she also rekindle the love of the boy's father?

***

Celebrate fatherhood—and love!—every month.
FABULOUS FATHERS...only in ♥ *Silhouette* ROMANCE™

Look us up on-line at: http://www.romance.net

FF-J-M

You're About to Become a *Privileged* *Woman*

Reap the rewards of fabulous free gifts and benefits with proofs-of-purchase from Silhouette and Harlequin books

Pages & Privileges™

It's our way of thanking you for buying our books at your favorite retail stores.

```
PROOF OF
PURCHASE            SR-PP21
Offer expires March 31, 1997
```

Harlequin and Silhouette— the most privileged readers in the world!

For more information about Harlequin and Silhouette's PAGES & PRIVILEGES program call the Pages & Privileges Benefits Desk: 1-503-794-2499

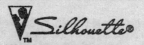

SR-PP21

COMING NEXT MONTH

#1204 DADDY BY DECISION—Lindsay Longford
Fabulous Fathers
Charming and sexy Jonas Riley had slipped past Jessica McDonald's
defenses years ago. Now the rancher was back—and proposing marriage
to the single mom. But would Jonas still want Jessica when he found
out the secret about her little boy?

#1205 IT'S RAINING GROOMS—Carolyn Zane
I'm Your Groom
Prudence was praying for a husband when rugged Trent Tanner literally
fell from above—through her ceiling! Though Trent was no answered
prayer, his request that she pose as his fiancée just might be the miracle
Prudence was looking for!

#1206 TO WED AGAIN?—DeAnna Talcott
I'm Your Groom
Once Mr. and Mrs., Meredith and Rowe Worth suddenly found themselves
adoptive parents to an adorable little girl. Now that they were learning to
bandage boo-boos and read bedtime stories, could they also learn to fall in
love and wed—again?

#1207 AN ACCIDENTAL MARRIAGE—Judith Janeway
I'm Your Groom
Best man Ryan Holt had never wanted to become a groom himself—
until a last-minute cover-up left everyone thinking he was married to
maid of honor Kit Kendrick! Now this confirmed bachelor was captivated
by lovely Kit and wished their "marriage" was no accident!

#1208 HUSBAND NEXT DOOR—Anne Ha
I'm Your Groom
When Shelly got engaged to a nice, stable, *boring* fiancé, Aaron Carpenter
suddenly realized he was in love with his beautiful neighbor, and set out to
convince her that he was her perfect husband—next door!

#1209 WEDDING RINGS AND BABY THINGS—Teresa Southwick
I'm Your Groom
To avoid scandal, single mom-to-be Kelly Walker needed a husband fast,
not forever. But after becoming Mrs. Mike Cameron, Kelly was soon
falling for this handsome father figure, and hoping for a family for always.